'Twas the week before Christmas,
When all through the house,
Not one soul was stirring—nary a creak in the house.
One child was snuggled under the blanket with care,
While two Angels hovered, awaiting hope and love for all to be shared.
The two Angels watched her sleeping
And knew without a doubt,
This Christmas would be remembered,
And so would the Christ Child, and his clout.
Though many had fogotten for many a year,
The true spirit of Christmas and its time was near.
And though this child was sleeping, the Angels knew
She'd bring back faith, and a love for Christmas, renewed.
And before they all slept on Christmas night,
They would hear Christ's whisper, bidding them a good night.
And above all, wishing them a Merry Christmas,
And to all a good life!

Also by Evie Rhodes

CRISS CROSS

EXPIRED

OUT "A" ORDER

STREET VENGEANCE

Published by Dafina Books

The FORGOTTEN SPIRIT

Evie Rhodes

Kensington Publishing Corp.
http://www.kensingtonbooks.com

DAFINA BOOKS are published by

Kensington Publishing Corp.
850 Third Avenue
New York, NY 10022

All Kensington Titles, Imprints, and Distributed Lines are available at special quantity discounts for bulk purchases for sales promotions, premiums, fund-raising, and educational or institutional use. Special book excerpts or customized printings can also be created to fit specific needs. For details, write or phone the office of the Kensington Special Sales Manager: Kensington Publishing Corp., 850 Third Avenue, New York, NY 10022, Attn: Special Sales Department. Phone: 1-800-221-2647.

Dafina and the Dafina logo Reg. U.S. Pat. & TM Off.

ISBN-13: 978-0-7582-2220-6
ISBN-10: 0-7582-2220-3

First trade paperback printing: October 2007
First mass market printing: October 2008

10 9 8 7 6 5 4 3 2 1

Printed in the United States of America

For My Lord,

Jesus Christ

ACKNOWLEDGMENTS

The Lord Jesus Christ—
You've given so much that I wish I had even more to give!

James Rhodes—
Thank you for seeing the vision.
And thank you for loving Jesus Christ enough to give all that you have!

My Express Gratitude to:

Selena James, Executive Editor Thank you for lending your editorial gift, and for your very special insight. Most of all thank you for being you!

Kristine Mills-Noble, Creative Director Thank you for creating a magnificent cover design. Most of all thank you for the gift of your adoring child gracing the cover!

The Child on the Cover Thank you for lending your beautiful spirit for the world to see!

Karen Thomas Thank you for believing and for championing this story to the forefront!

Kensington Publishing Corporation (The Dafina Imprint) Thank you for your excitement and the publishing of *The Forgotten Spirit: A Christmas Tale*! Most of all, thank you for giving it your best!

Robert G. (Bob) Diforio, Literary Agent Thank you for your assistance in the placement of this story! Most of all I'd like to thank you for your graciousness.

Rozzie Lee Jackson, My Mother Gone. But never forgotten. Thank you for helping me to know I have a gift. But most of all, thank you for leaving me a great legacy—the sharing of the knowledge of the Lord Jesus Christ!

Pearl Peyton, Jimmy's Grandmother Gone. But never forgotten. I know you'd be just so proud to see that the boy you raised has become a great man. You are loved and missed by Jimmy more than you could ever know! Much love from me to you. I'm reaping the blessings with the grandson you helped to raise.

James Rhodes, Jr. Thank you for your sacrifice of my time that you've given up so that others might have this story!

Jamie Lynne Rhodes Thank you for being the namesake for the little girl in this story!

My Sisters Josephine Shannon, Eva Shannon, and Joy Shannon You're my girls! You always have been and you always will be! Keep the faith!

My Youngest Uncles Robert Jackson, Jr., Robin Jackson, and Reginald Jackson I'll always cherish our Christmases together and our childhood memories. Much love!

Linda Lepp I thank the Lord for second chances. Here is my chance to get this right. I thank you for believing in me. I thank you for the unselfish love you've shown. And I thank you for being a most special friend. I'd also like to thank you for the gift of the Museum Pen with which I signed my first writing contract. But most of all I thank you for your sharing, and giving and for showing me your joy in giving! You will never know how much I miss your presence in my life.

Eleanor Tafari-Best My special Queen Mother, who is a tower of dignity and who exemplifies what strength of character is really about. To you and your son, Joel David Best, I dedicate my chapter entitled "The Summons" for sharing with me the power in how you've seen past Jo Best's handicap, and looked into his very special spirit leading you both to an extraordinary path of life. May the Lord Bless you. I love you truly!

Nukilwa Taquilaya, Family Thanks to you and Evelyn for sharing with Jimmy and me what family, history, and love is really about. And thank you for your contributions to the dream. Most of all thank you for always being a great dad to me as well as for always being there for me. I love you!

Alfred A. Arico, Family Truly I could never say enough so I'll keep it simple. I cherish every memory with you. And I thank you for being there for me as well as for all of life's lessons that you've taught me. And for loving me as your own. I love you truly!

Cleo Duke-Wright Thank you for being you. You are a very special lady!

Family & Friends It is impossible to name you all individually but know that you are always wished the salvation and the love of the Lord Jesus Christ!

Childhood Friends Thank you for being you. Both those who are here, and those who are not. And thank you for contributing poignancy to both the life of Jimmy Rhodes and myself.

RIP (Rest in Peace) For Our Friends in Hartford Who Are No Longer with Us Jimmy and I shall always remember you! And you will forever remain in our hearts.

The City of Hartford and Its Residents James Rhodes and I would like to thank you for being the model city in the story of *The Forgotten Spirit.* More than that thank you for our memories; without them we wouldn't be who we are!

The Reader Thank you for reading! You're a treasure in my life.

The Unsung Heroes Thank you; I know you're out there!

And Last But Not Least The story of *The Forgotten Spirit: A Christmas Tale* is for you, and you, and you, and you!

For All Those Who Know Me I Remain as Always Standing in the Spirit!

For God so loved the world, that he gave His only begotten Son, that whosoever believeth in him should not perish, but have everlasting life.

—John 3:16

Prologue

'Twas the week before Christmas and all through the house, not one soul was stirring, there wasn't even a creak in the house. One child was snuggled under the blanket with care, while two angels prepared kindling, the Christ Child, and his birth soon to be shared.

There was a mystique that hung in the air, for the angels knew power and truth would be declared!

"He was born in a manger," said the one angel.

"She's born in the hood," said the other.

"There's not too much difference," said the first.

"Hmmm," replied the other.

The sleeping girl child snuggled deeper under her blanket. She wasn't even aware of the silver crystals being sprinkled around her head, nor did she have knowledge of the two angels who watched her sleeping, and who received the nod of approval regarding her innocence.

This Christmas everything would be different.

"Did you forget something?" asked the first angel.

"I haven't forgotten anything," replied the other. "But they did."

The first angel let that go for now. They were

here because *they* had forgotten. Instead he asked, "What about the mother?"

The other angel pointed.

Looking toward the bureau they saw a beautiful Christmas ornament as the first angel beheld what the other angel meant.

A scene unfolded revealing a federal prison. He could see the army of little child angels loaded with their silver sawdust, heads bent in determination, surrounding a woman's cell.

A cloud of sawdust circled her head like a halo. She never stirred. Neither did the sleeping child.

Silent night.

As the two angels walked down the trash-strewn, wind-blown street, the other said to the first, "Why are we walking? We don't have to you know."

"Neither did the spirit of the Christ Child have to come to this neighborhood, but he did."

"Hmmm," was the only reply that was heard.

What It Could Have Been

It could have been the night before Christmas, instead it 'twas a night not to be forgotten. A night not recorded through various fantasies, such as *The Night Before Christmas,* a story that burns brightly in most people's minds. It was a night of great importance nonetheless, but with much less fanfare.

It was a night directly linked to the Christ Child, and the truth surrounding his birth. All in all, it was a night that would touch the hearts of those who truly needed it.

A people who needed to remember the forgotten spirit.

As the celebrations in all their gaiety resounded throughout the world and masses of people spilled into the streets beginning their celebrations of Christmas, the hushed silence in this particular realm was in startling contrast as one child was sprinkled with the stardust of remembrance.

It was a remembrance that went beyond the gaily wrapped packages, the decorated trees, and the stockings hung by the chimneys with care. And, of course, beyond the steady chi-ching of cash registers at retailers around the world.

And, it was not a myth. It was truth in all its power. It was wondrous, magnificent, and joyous in its giving. It was in its essence, the greatest love of all.

And on this night one small child, parallel in circumstances, though not in holiness, to a night many eons ago would receive a charge. One that was much bigger than she was at nine years old.

Hartford, Connecticut, was renowned as the Insurance Capital of the World. Little did its citizens know that after this night, it would become known as so much more.

The city of Hartford had been imbued with a spiritual, magical realism along with some very special visitors. And, the footprints of those visitors had been recorded, recorded in a place where it would be most remembered.

Deep in the heart of the city, in a modest two-family home, nine-year-old Jamie Lynne Brooks knelt with her ear to the dining room door. Though she was dressed warmly in flannel pajamas, she still shivered more from the sound of the voices, coming from the other side of the door, than from the cold.

A bright, precocious, and curious child, sometimes Jamie tried to learn more than she should. Just as she was doing now, which is why she found herself suddenly fleeing down the hall, with a guilty expression on her face, while she softly closed the door after reaching the safety of her room.

The following morning Jamie's grandmother, Elizabeth Brooks, prepared the same breakfast that she had been preparing the week before Christmas, for more years than she could remember.

There was bacon, as well as smoked ham shipped from Virginia. It was a special catalog order that arrived every year, along with gourmet sausage links.

Elizabeth, or Lizzie as she was sometimes called, had prepared buttermilk pancakes. She had wheat as well as banana nut pancakes, served with old-fashioned maple syrup warmed to perfection.

There were platters of eggs as well as a vast assortment of honey and apple and original butters that Lizzie collected from around the country.

Fresh-baked strawberry scones sat in baskets wrapped in colorful cloths, along with a vast array of marmalades, jams, and jellies.

In the center of the table was a bowl of fresh fruit.

Each day leading up to Christmas morning would bring a variety of breakfast dishes, sumptuous enough for a king, and certainly worthy of the Prince of Prince's birthday.

The Christmas lights that hung from the gaily decorated tree in the dining room tinkled *Joy to the World,* softly in the background.

Elizabeth Brooks was a stickler for tradition, and Christmas was the one time of the year when she didn't feel the least bit guilty for sticking to what others liked to call her regimen. She always did exactly what she felt like to make Christmas the most festive of occasions.

She looked over to see that the coffee had finished brewing. She poured a steaming cup from the gleaming red Kitchen-Aid coffeepot for her husband George who began the morning conversation exactly where he had left off the night before, which was what had sent Jamie scurrying to her room, in tears.

"I just don't know how I'm going to tell Jamie her mother won't be home for Christmas."

Elizabeth automatically poured cream into George's cup. "Hmmm. Hmmm. It's going to break her heart all right."

George spooned in the sugar.

Elizabeth sighed. "Well now, George, let's not give up so soon. Maybe something will happen."

The scowl on George's face deepened. Worry lines creased his forehead. "Oh sure it will. The Connecticut Parole Board will get a touch of the Christmas spirit, and release her."

Elizabeth ignored his sarcasm. She put a buttered scone on his plate.

"It's the week before Christmas for goodness sake."

He turned his attention back to the morning paper, exasperated. Unable to read as he felt Elizabeth's eyes assessing him he glanced up.

"You know I've been married to you for what feels like forever. And I can't believe you of all people would go and make a remark like that, Lizzie," he said, using his nickname for her.

Elizabeth rolled her eyes but refused to change her position.

"Maybe nothing will happen like nothing is happening. You can't go filling a child's head with that kind of nonsense. Kids have to learn to live in reality."

"Ain't nothing wrong with having a little faith," Elizabeth said.

George finally snapped his paper shut.

"Ain't nothing wrong with living in reality either. Which is where we live most of the time. And the reality is that nothing good ever seems to happen around here."

Elizabeth refused to be deterred from her hope.

Sighing again she whispered, "What we need is a miracle."

Jamie Lynne Brooks

Jamie sat on the window seat in her room staring at a photograph of her mother. Tears trickled slowly down her cheeks. "Please, God, let her come home."

Her heart felt heavy, as though it were too big for her chest. She could actually feel the weight of it. And it felt as though it weighed a ton.

She glanced out the window. Jamie loved to sit and watch the huge soft flakes of snow drift to the ground. But there wasn't even a snowflake floating in the air to cheer her up. The streets were cold, dry, windy, and barren. There wasn't a sign of snow in sight.

She ran her fingers over the photograph of her mother, Cynthia Brooks. She missed her mother and the thought of no snow saddened her even further. She loved this time of year, the smells, the sounds, the feel of the snow in the air, the warmth of family.

But this Christmas would be different.

Her mother would not be there to tuck her into bed, sing her a song, or to sneak her cookies and milk from Grandma Lizzie's kitchen.

One would think she would have gotten used to it by now because Cynthia hadn't been there for the last three years.

Nevertheless Jamie was harboring memories of their Christmases past, and yearning for the touch of her mother, whose incarceration was far beyond her young reach.

Jamie looked out the window as the sounds of boys playing touch football reached her ears. She sat on the bench hugging the picture of her mother while she watched the boys toss the football and tackle each other.

In the living room George was sitting in his favorite recliner, a chair forbidden to all others. The chair fit his body like a glove; it hugged the very imprint of him filling him with satisfaction.

Lizzie had started a fire in the fireplace and its crackling flames filled the room with warmth. The sparkling Christmas tree in the dining room added to the holiday glow. A beautiful gold star was perched proudly on top.

George was feeling rather satisfied from the wonderful breakfast Lizzie had prepared. He was about to light his pipe when Jamie climbed into his lap, putting her arms around his neck. She lay her head against the warm spot beating in his throat.

He hadn't heard her come into the room. Sometimes she reminded him of an angel appearing, and disappearing, at will. It wasn't that she could do that, but she put him in that frame of mind sometimes, as she came and went so quietly you barely knew she was there.

George laid his pipe in the ashtray without lighting it. He cradled her in his arms. "I'm sorry, baby. Granddaddy did everything he could think of to bring your mommy home for Christmas. But, well, it just can't be. I'm sorry, baby. I'm truly sorry."

Recovering from her own sadness, and still hopeful as well as unable to accept the truth of her grandfather's words, Jamie asked, "Isn't there anything that anyone can do?"

She looked down at the floor as she felt a lump forming in her throat.

Then she turned big brown eyes filled with unshed tears directly on him, scrutinizing his every feature for the slightest twitch.

Her hair was braided with beautiful beads woven through, and the hair was pulled away from her face, so her granddaddy got the full frontal impact of the pain emanating from Jamie.

Seeing the earnestness on her face he answered directly. "I'm afraid not, Jamie."

He refused to give her false hope. He had spoken to the attorney as well as to representatives of various organizations, who in turn had spoken with prison officials, and through it all he had received a very firm *no* for an answer.

His daughter would not be home for Christmas.

"Are you sure, Granddaddy, that not anyone anywhere can do anything?" Jamie persisted.

George sighed.

He wanted to light his pipe badly but couldn't do so with Jamie sitting on his lap. He loved his grandchild dearly but sometimes she wore him out with her stream of questions and her never-ending ability to *not* accept no for an answer.

"I'm sure. I wish I wasn't but I am."

Jamie looked at him before sliding off his lap. She gazed briefly into the fireplace, and then tilted her head at a proud angle. "Don't worry, Granddaddy. I know you did your best. It's okay, really. Everything will be all right. I promise."

She smiled brightly, like the sun appearing on a cloudy day. She hugged him tightly, absorbing his disappointment in her little body.

Putting her hand under his chin she forced his downcast eyes to look into hers. "Remember don't look down or wear a frown. Life is like a jeweled crown for those who see, and have found."

Jamie loved reciting poetry that she'd made up, and times like these were when the poetry cheered her up.

For his part her grandfather wondered where she got her wisdom for one so young. It sprouted from her at odd times.

She put a finger to her lips and then touched the same finger to his lips; leaning over she kissed him on the nose. "Can I go outside, Granddaddy?"

"Sure thing, muffin." He tickled her and she fell to the floor in a gale of giggles. It was one of their favorite pastimes.

"But first we're going to have to take you to

the hospital and get some of those funny bones taken out."

Elizabeth smiled at them from the kitchen.

Wistfully she repeated her wish. "All we need is a miracle."

Hattie Brooks

Jamie was excited to be on Christmas vacation. There was so much to do, things to see and places to go. The only shadow marring her thoughts was her mother's absence.

She decided to visit her great-grandmother, which she usually did on the weekends.

Armed with a platter of warm pancakes from Grandma Lizzie's breakfast table, Jamie pushed insistently on Hattie Brooks' bell until the buzzer sounded to let her in. Her great-grandmother lived just a few houses up the street.

Jamie bolted through the door and up the stairs. She was about to bang on the front door when her great-grandmother, leaning heavily on her cane, opened it.

"Well for land sakes, child, you gonna take the door off the hinges, the way you did that buzzer down there."

Jamie grinned. With her empty arm she hugged her great-grandmother around her waist.

"I'm sorry, Grandma, I just wanted to see you so badly."

The old woman melted.

"Why of course you did, child. Come on in here and take off those cold clothes."

Jamie smiled.

She loved this old woman with all her heart. She always called Hattie Grandma even though Hattie was her great-grandmother, and her grandmother was always called Grandma Lizzie.

Nobody who knew Hattie and Lizzy would ever confuse them. Lizzie was charming, warm, gracious, and full of fun and wit, which actually sometimes grated on Hattie's nerves.

Hattie was serious, all observant and tough, except when it came to Jamie. Hattie Brooks was Jamie's grandfather's mother. And she had been a pistol in her day, and still was most of the time. However Jamie had her wrapped around her finger.

It had been so since the day George had brought Jamie home, and she had looked down at that beautiful baby, wrapped in the scraggly pink blanket.

Hattie of course had known from the day Jamie's mother Cynthia was born that she would be trouble. She'd just had that air about her. However, George was her only son, and he loved his daughter to death, so how could she tell him that?

Instead she had observed—silently—Cynthia's spoiled selfishness. Her heart filled with sorrow every time Cynthia did something that proved her right.

As much as Elizabeth got on her nerves, sometimes Hattie wished Cynthia had taken a bit more of her disposition.

Instead, Cynthia had an edge. She loved what old folks used to call "the hustle." Something always seemed to be brewing with her, most of the time none of it was good, with the exception of the birth of Jamie Lynne Brooks.

Hattie knew Jamie was a different package altogether. She was not remotely like her mother in any way. Hattie didn't know how Cynthia had been blessed with a child of such a good spirit.

But praise the Lord for his miracles.

Hattie headed for her favorite chair. It must have been in the genes in their family because her son did the same thing every day.

Mahalia Jackson's distinctive notes sailed through the air as Hattie settled herself in for a chat with her favorite girl-child.

Seated in her rocking chair by the window she indicated the big fluffy pillow at her feet.

Jamie had been sitting on that pillow at her feet since she was old enough to sit up. When she hadn't been old enough to sit up, Hattie used to prop her up with extra pillows.

Laying her cane against the windowsill Hattie's eyes probed Jamie's face. "Now tell me child what is the trouble that I see in those beautiful brown eyes that has you in such a rush?"

"Granddaddy told me Mommy won't be here for Christmas. They won't let her come. Grandma, she was all I wanted for Christmas. I don't have to have toys or clothes. All I want is my mommy. She's been gone a long time."

Hattie watched Jamie closely.

Before a tear could drop from her eye she handed her a handkerchief. "Granddaddy said not anyone anywhere could do anything."

Hattie opened her arms beckoning to her. "Come child. Come on over here to Grandma. That pillow you're sitting on is too far away."

Jamie went to her. She laid her head in her great-grandmother's lap. Hattie stroked the child's hair comforting her. She glanced over the top of Jamie's head to the wooden cross hanging on the wall. "I know someone who can help you."

Jamie lifted her head from the wet spot she'd left on her Grandmother's apron. "Who?"

"Jesus."

"You mean God?"

"No I mean Jesus just like I said. You can't approach God unless you go through his son Jesus. In the name of the Almighty Jesus you can do all things. And through him you can talk to God."

Jamie looked puzzled.

"You know how to use the phone, child. Don't you?"

"Yes."

"Well when you pick up the receiver you punch in a number and that becomes the line you use. It rings on the other end and someone answers and you start talking. Right?"

"Right."

"Well Jesus is like that line you punched in. He's the way, the truth, and the life, child. He said there's no other way but through me. And he meant what he said all right. Through him you can reach God. When you respect the name of Jesus, God picks up on the other end, and he answers."

Jamie puckered her lips considering this information.

"Do you understand me, child?"

"Yes. Yes, Grandma, I do."

Drifting for a moment Hattie said in a faraway voice, "Jesus is the light of the world. He's powerful. He's also a miracle worker."

"I overheard Grandma Lizzie say what we need is a miracle. Just this morning she said it to Granddaddy. A miracle can bring my mommy home."

Smiling fondly Hattie said, "Yes, baby it can. You see Jesus helped the lame to walk, the dumb to talk, and the blind to see. He came for you and me."

Jamie looked across at her. "You just made a rhyme Grandma."

"No I didn't, baby; that's just what the scripture says is all."

After a few seconds of reflection Hattie continued, "There is nothing he can't do. No job is too hard for him, Jamie. Do you know where he was born?"

"No."

"He was born in what we know as a barn. Back then they called it a manger. But it was a barn all right."

Jamie shook her head incredulously. "A barn? I thought you said he was powerful, Grandma."

Outside on a tree branch a child angel fell from the tree, where he had been eavesdropping, landing with a loud thump on the ground.

His partner, an angel known as the Spirit of Discernment who had been waiting on the ground, looked at him, shaking his head for naught.

"That's what you get." Discernment was annoyed because they could've just sat inside the room listening without either the old woman or the child being aware of them, if they had chose to.

Instead Sam, known as the Spirit of Innocence, in his usual way, wanted to experience the physical. That was why he had fallen. He wasn't quite used to how gravity worked.

Brushing himself off and getting back to the matter at hand, Sam said, "The old woman is getting every word of it right."

The Spirit of Discernment sighed.

Sam, as he was most often called instead of by his angelic name, was renowned for answering questions he hadn't yet been asked.

Discernment knew that just as children in the flesh could be precocious so could little child angels. Sam was nine years old, the same age as Jamie.

Inside Hattie said, "He was, and still remains powerful, Jamie. Still waters run deep."

She gazed out the window as though she could see the two angels, who were now perched together on a tree limb. Sam usually got his way with Discernment.

"The time of his birth is approaching," Hattie said. "He is the Savior. And he will grant a miracle, or miracles, on one condition."

Jamie grasped the bottom of her grandma's

apron, intent on what she was saying, gazing at her. "What's that, Grandma? What's the condition?"

Her great-grandmother stared at her as though she were searching for something.

Finally speaking softly she said, "The condition is that you *must* believe. No matter what anyone tells you, or how hard it may get. No matter how impossible it may seem, child. You've got to believe that whatever you ask in Jesus' name will be. It's called faith, Jamie. You must believe, child. You've just got to believe."

Jamie leaped to her feet.

"I believe, Grandma. I do," she said earnestly. A shiver passed through her body as she spoke the words.

"I gotta go. I'll be back," she told her great-grandmother. With those words she kissed Hattie on the cheek, dashing from the room.

She stopped when she was halfway out of the room, looking at the old woman, whose eyes were bright and shiny.

"Grandma, how come Granddaddy doesn't know about Jesus and him being a miracle worker?"

Her voice dropped to a whisper. "I know you're right. And I know Jesus can help. I know it cuz I feel it right here." She pointed to her heart.

Hattie shook her head sadly. "He knows, Jamie. Many people know. It's just that they've forgotten."

A tear rolled down the old woman's cheek.

Outside on the tree limb the two angels wiped their eyes, as well knowing what was coming.

"Baby, Jesus Christ is the forgotten spirit. People have forgotten what Christmas is really about. Perhaps you can help them remember."

In a voice that belied her years, Jamie answered, "Perhaps I can, Grandma."

She pulled on her hat and coat heading for the door, closing it softly behind her.

Hattie rocked in her chair, humming along with the Christmas spirituals.

Outside Hattie's window the tree limb was empty.

Cynthia Brooks

Cynthia Brooks was going to lose her mind if the constant dripping didn't stop.

The sound of the water was driving her crazy, not to mention the blackness surrounding her. She couldn't see her hand in front of her face.

She sighed heavily.

It was close to time for her release from prison. She had been hoping to be home with her daughter for Christmas, until she wound up in a fight that landed her in this godforsaken hole in a prison in Danbury. A fight that she hadn't started.

She heard something scurrying and drew her body into a tighter ball, her arms hugging her knees. The sound of her own breathing was her only company.

She was in federal prison because of writing bad checks. After this incarceration she decided she'd never again sign her name to a check.

What was to be a quick and easy dollar had cost her three years of her life, as well as a hefty fine, bail money, and attorney's fees, all paid by her father.

And that was only time and money. She couldn't begin to calculate the loss to her daughter. The thought cut as though a knife had been shoved in her heart.

For all of Cynthia's street smarts she knew Jamie wasn't like most children. She knew the Lord had blessed her with a special gift in her child.

She'd known it and ignored it.

Cynthia pinched herself until she cried. Role playing, she talked to herself so she could hear the sound of a human voice.

"You know you shouldn't have done it," the sterner of her voices admonished.

"What's done is done," replied the weaker voice.

"Yeah. You're what is done all right. Thrown away in this forgotten hole!"

Suddenly the pain of being *forgotten* swamped her. She could no longer speak.

Could she live with not being remembered?

The Spirit of Innocence turned to look up at the Spirit of Discernment. "Does she have to stay?" Sam asked, his voice heavy with emotion.

Discernment shook his head. "For now I'm afraid she does."

The black hole that Cynthia was locked in became blacker. The only sounds heard were her whimpers and the constant drip of the water.

What Cynthia didn't know was that the Lord's

spirit had resided on the face of the water, in the deep since the beginning of time, long before the creation of the earth and man.

The water was consistent in both rhyme and reason.

Mr. Mitchell

Jamie skipped along the street past the neighborhood houses and stores. She smiled her hellos to the shopkeepers along the way. They smiled and waved, most smitten with this always smiling child.

Jamie's cheerfulness was contagious.

Mr. Mitchell, one of Hartford's icons, watched Jamie skipping along. His grocery store had been in the same location for as long as anyone could remember. The store was special, like having a spot of country and home rolled into one, and Mr. Mitchell was such a character some people shopped there simply for a dose of his special brand of hospitality. He was warm, quick witted, and giving. And his store gave off a warmth of atmosphere that embraced you, inviting you into its special world with its sawdust floor and candy cane smells.

He waved to Jamie and she skipped over to him smiling. "Good morning, Mr. Mitchell."

"Good morning yourself, Jamie girl." He glanced at his watch, and then looked at Jamie. "Well it's barely good morning. It's almost noon now."

Looking up Mr. Mitchell said, "Shame it ain't gonna be no snow this Christmas. I guess I'm just plain old-fashioned, always dreaming of a white snowy Christmas."

Jamie giggled.

Sighing, he turned to go into the store. When Jamie didn't move he said, "Come on in. I got a bag of goodies for you. You don't need to stand there freezing while you listen to an old man's ramblings."

"You're not old, Mr. Mitchell."

"I'm older than dirt, Jamie."

Jamie frowned. "How old is dirt?" she asked seriously.

This time Mr. Mitchell giggled. He'd forgotten how on point Jamie could be.

"Never mind, Jamie Lynne," he said, drawing her name out. "Just suffice it to say I'm old enough."

Jamie followed him into the store.

She slipped off her mittens and cap and climbed on top of the barrel sitting on sawdust on the floor. She looked around at the array of Christmas decorations—candy apples and peppermint sticks hanging from strings, and huge red lollipops on the counter, and the smell of cinnamon was in the air.

Miz Taylor, who was Jamie's neighbor, came

into the store, stomped her feet from the cold and loosened her scarf, then removed her gloves.

"Good day, Miz Taylor. Is it cold enough for you?" Mr. Mitchell said by way of a greeting.

Miz Taylor walked past Jamie briefly pausing to pinch her cheeks. "It's cold enough I tell you."

She turned back, chucking Jamie under the chin. "Hello, Jamie Lynne."

Jamie glanced at Mr. Mitchell to see if he was going to rescue her. The mischievous gleam in his eye told her he was not. He only shrugged and smiled, leaving her to contend with Miz Taylor, who was the neighborhood's busybody.

Jamie asked, "Hello, Miz Taylor. How are you today?"

Miz Taylor, eyeing Jamie as a hen would a tasty bug, replied "Well I guess you could say I'm fine. How's your Granddaddy?"

As an afterthought she added, "Oh, and of course your grandmamma?" She gave Jamie a tolerant little smile.

"They're both fine, Miz Taylor. I'll tell them you asked," Jamie said.

Mr. Mitchell did all he could to hide a smile because Miz Taylor looked stricken at Jamie's response, which glazed right past her hidden meanings.

Flustered, but gathering her presence of mind, Miz Taylor replied, "You be sure and do that now."

Mr. Mitchell occupied himself with dusting off his pristinely kept jelly jars until Miz Taylor was ready to place her order.

Still focusing on Jamie, she said, "I bet you're waiting for Santa Claus to bring you lots of presents."

Mr. Mitchell rolled his eyes heavenward. No child in the ghetto past the age of four believed in Santa Claus.

He smiled because he knew if any child could handle Miz Taylor it was Jamie Lynne. No sooner than the thought entered his mind than Jamie said in all seriousness, "No, ma'am. I'm not waiting for Santa Claus. I'm waiting for Jesus to bring me a miracle."

Miz Taylor was so startled by Jamie's reply her hand flew to her throat. Mr. Mitchell bit back a smile.

"Oh my . . . well now . . . hmmm. I see." Flustered she turned to Mr. Mitchell who graciously decided to rescue her.

"Miz Taylor, what can I get for you on this fine day?"

Jamie turned her attention to the beautiful glass ball with snow and a house sitting inside it. She shook it, watching the snowflakes fall over the house.

"I need some sweet potatoes for my pies, Paul. And give me the best ones you got. I can't be using no inferior sweet potatoes in my pie." Everyone in town knew that Mr. Mitchell carried the best sweet potatoes for miles around but anyone listening to Miz Taylor would have thought his goods were not the best grade.

"I'm gonna be baking some sweet potato pies for the shelter again this year. I need plenty of them. I'll take some cinnamon, nutmeg, and vanilla flavoring, too."

Mr. Mitchell loaded the potatoes on the scale as Jamie slid off the barrel on which she'd been sitting. She went to the window. She gazed at the sky, then she absently took in the scenery on the street.

When the sale was complete, Miz Taylor walked past Jamie on her way out of the door. When she opened it, bells chimed. "Have a good day, Jamie Lynne."

"You, too, Miz Taylor."

As the woman started out the door Jamie said, "Miz Taylor."

"Yes?"

Jamie gave Mr. Mitchell a sly look. She pointed above the door and smiled. "You're standing under the mistletoe." She turned wide almond shaped eyes on Miz Taylor.

In a huff, Miz Taylor stepped through the door. "Whoever taught you such nonsense, child? For goodness sakes." The door slammed behind her. The bells continued to chime. Mr. Mitchell rolled his eyes.

Laughing he said, "Jamie, you are full of mischief."

"But you don't have a wife and Miz Taylor doesn't have a husband."

Mr. Mitchell pulled a mock-angry face. "And you're not gonna have a treat or a backside if you keep this up, young lady."

Jamie skipped back to the barrel and returned to her perch. "Okay, Mr. Mitchell. But Miz Taylor bakes the best sweet potato pies this side of the Mississippi and everybody knows that."

"Yep. And every year she drops one off for me because of those excellent sweet potatoes I give her and I prefer to keep it that way." Together they laughed.

Mr. Mitchell picked Jamie up, standing her on top of the barrel. Then he perched against the counter. "Now let's hear that song you sang in the Christmas play. I wanna hear my own special version. Your granddaddy told me it was great."

Jamie looked slightly embarrassed. "No it wasn't, Mr. Mitchell. He's my granddaddy. He thinks it's good no matter what."

"And so do I. Now start singing, child, and share that good spirit the Lord gave you."

"Well. Okay."

Jamie sang *Joy to the World* in her childish voice. When she finished, she stretched out her arms wide as though she were on the Radio City Music Hall stage. Mr. Mitchell lifted her from atop the barrel, placing her gently on the floor.

He clapped and clapped and clapped.

"Now that is exactly what I needed. You made my day." He went behind the counter and pulled out a brown paper bag decorated with different color bows. Jamie's name was written in script across the bag.

He sat it on the counter as Jamie watched with a smile on her face. "There's to be no peeking out of you, young lady."

Jamie reached for the bag. He pulled it back. "I mean it."

She giggled. "I know."

"You're gonna open it as soon as you get out of my sight."

This time full-scale laughter erupted from Jamie. "Yes. You know I am."

He handed her the bag, rolling his eyes as he did so.

Inquisitively, Jamie asked, "Why do you think there ain't going to be any snow this Christmas, Mr. Mitchell?"

"Don't use the word ain't. It's isn't." He used *ain't* all the time but it was important to him that Jamie used proper grammar. He was too old to change his ways. Besides, he liked the way he talked. But Jamie was going places in life so she needed to present herself in the right light.

"Why do you think there isn't going to be any snow this Christmas?" she corrected herself.

"Don't rightly know, Jamie. It's just a prediction, I guess."

"Well, I think I might know how to get some snow if you really want it."

Taken aback, Mr. Mitchell said, "You want to tell me how."

She shook her head. "No. Not right now. If you believe it, it will come. We'll have plenty of snow, you'll see."

Mr. Mitchell's eyes twinkled.

Jamie leaned over hugging him tightly. Then she headed for the door. When she was almost there she turned back beckoning to him. "I almost forgot."

She pulled a small gaily wrapped package from her pocket and handed it to him.

"Merry Christmas, Mr. Mitchell."

Mr. Mitchell looked up. He pointed to the mistletoe. Jamie grinned. He planted a kiss on her cheek and then she was gone.

Mr. Mitchell opened the box she'd given him to find a tiny cross nestled inside. He looked up with watery eyes watching Jamie skip down the street, as she peeked in the bag he'd given her.

Heading back to the counter he saw a brief flash of mist and then it disappeared. It was so quick, he blinked unsure he had even really seen what he'd thought he'd seen.

He could have sworn he'd seen a little boy child stumbling over his feet.

The Lesson

Sam and the Spirit of Discernment stood in the midst of a very dark cemetery, known in the city as the Ancient Burying Ground.

It was the oldest historic site in Hartford, and the only one surviving from the 1600s. From 1640 until the early 1800s it was Hartford's only graveyard.

For as far as the eye could see there were tombstones with distinctive art and gravestone carvings. Low-hanging branches complemented the whistle in the air.

Sam looked up at the Spirit of Discernment. At nine years of age he was at the very beginning of angelhood and most things about the human condition were new for him.

Shivering, he pulled his jacket a little tighter and asked, "Why are we here?"

The Spirit of Discernment didn't appear to be cold at all. He was wearing his physicality well. He turned to Sam. "We are here, little one, because before one can embrace the present or future one must first take a look at the roots of the past. That is where most things are shaped."

Sam considered this. "But I thought we were shaping things now."

Discernment shook his head. Once again he was reminded that child angels in many ways weren't so different from ordinary children. "Sam, the path we're on has already been shaped by the past. Just as those we are here to shine the light on have been shaped by their pasts."

Sam heard footsteps, but when he looked around he saw no one. Discernment knew the representation of those footsteps would leave a mark, a mark in the spirit. He also knew that it meant that the one to whom those footprints belonged had been carrying them.

He had carried them by his blood.

"Come, Sam. We must get started." As if on cue, they heard a repetitive *ka-chunk*, the sound of a shovel hitting dirt, and dirt hitting a coffin.

Sam knew that wasn't good. Dirt hitting a coffin could only mean one thing—something, or more likely someone, was dead and being buried.

They were gasping for breath by the time they arrived in the area of the sound. The noise had sounded very close, but it was in actuality nearly at the other end of the cemetery.

Looking into the hole, Sam saw a glass coffin almost covered with dirt, except for the top half. As he gazed through the glass, a startled little whimper escaped him as he recognized the face of Jamie Lynne Brooks.

Sam turned immediately to the Spirit of Discernment. "Oh no! I thought it was my job to help her."

"It is."

Bewildered, Sam yelped while wishing that that man would stop throwing dirt on the little girl in the glass coffin. "I can't! She's dead!"

Unperturbed, Discernment said, "You can. She's alive."

Sam protested. He jumped up and down in despair and frustration. He knew he was acting like a kid. Well he was a kid, sort of, but he wasn't supposed to be acting like one. Still jumping up and down, he pointed out a simple fact.

"But she's dead."

"Things are not always what they appear to be, Sam. The Jamie that you see in this coffin has already paid the price so that the one you know can live and go on to share the love."

As Sam watched, the image of the dead child changed to that of a small lamb. Its representation was of the one who had really paid the price for all, with his blood, and with his life. Jesus Christ.

The Spirit of Innocence knew he had just come by a hard-earned lesson. A lesson that was certainly more befitting of his angelic name.

"Come," said Discernment. "We have quite a night ahead."

Sam was silent as he was led to a tombstone that would prove to be only the first of his learnings.

The Spirit of Holiness

Sam was walking behind Discernment, trying to keep up when he stumbled. He was a clumsy little angel at times.

As his foot became entangled in the vines and weeds covering the ground, foliage that looked as though it could have been there for centuries prior to his and Discernment's arrival triggered a release; and before Sam's startled eyes, a tombstone rose from its depths.

After its slow ascent, it stood as an imposing sentinel. Written in a powerful slash across its face was, *Thou shalt have no other Gods before me.*

Sam uttered the words aloud.

Instantly, he and Discernment were repositioned to a vantage point from which they viewed the very origin of this particular sin.

What they saw went as far back as the exodus

out of Egypt at the time the people were worshipping a golden calf.

Fast-forwarded through time they saw the steady worsening of this sin.

With each passing century, the people embraced many concepts and things of the flesh, but not of the spirit.

And in each instance, Sam and Discernment witnessed the Spirit of Holiness abandoned.

In fact, the Spirit of Holiness stood off to the side while object after object, and eventually man after man took its place. These things were sought after—*he* was not.

Sam watched as the Spirit of Holiness was pushed aside until it was little more than a memory. He squinted, straining to see the remnants of the spirit.

He turned to the Spirit of Discernment with tears in his eyes. "What happened?"

Before Discernment could utter a word, they again heard the familiar *ka-chunk* of the shovel.

Once again they were back in the cemetery. Looking down into the glass coffin, this time Sam saw the Spirit of Holiness. The gravedigger shoveled in another mound of dirt.

Sam's heart lurched. "No!"

The last of the dirt hit the coffin. Holiness had been buried.

The Spirit of Discernment sighed. He knew that after this, Little Sam, the child Spirit of Innocence, would never again be the same. Innocence in all of its pureness could only be acquired at great cost.

It could only be maintained if it was *written*.

Before they could even turn away, the grave with Holiness in it, lying in a buried state, was sealed in for all its glory.

It was sealed as well as forgotten.

8

Eyes Wide Open

Hattie Brooks paused in the middle of her nightly ritual. Staring at her lathered face in the mirror, she spoke to her reflection. "These old bones are getting tired and weary, Jesus." This was something she would say only in the privacy of her own home. To the outside world, she displayed nothing but spunk and regalness.

She rinsed her face and reached for a towel to pat it dry. Laying the towel aside, she looked back to the mirror and beheld a mirage in place of her reflection. The mirage shimmered as though it couldn't hold all that it contained.

It was an image Hattie had seen before.

Hattie wasn't afraid. She had been seeing things since she was a child. The old folks in her time used to call it sleepwalking, for lack of a better term. But she knew it wasn't sleepwalking—she hadn't gone to bed and her eyes were wide open.

She leaned forward and stared hard at the undulating image until she made out the shape of her great-granddaughter, Jamie.

It had begun when Jamie was a baby. One night just prior to bed, Hattie had touched the scraggily pink blanket well used by Jamie, discarded by Lizzie, and rescued by Hattie.

In that blanket, as tattered and torn as it was, had lived the spirit that had loved as well as protected Jamie Lynne from the day she was born.

Hattie had retrieved it from the garbage can where her daughter-in-law Lizzie had thrown it, never to be seen again or so she'd thought. Lizzie didn't know about things of the spirit and such.

The first time Hattie touched the tattered blanket she had seen Jamie lying in the makeshift crib that Cynthia had fashioned from a cheap basket. She was wrapped in that scraggily pink blanket, but she wasn't alone. Stumbling next to her basket to get a better look at her was a child who looked to be about nine years old. With a shock, Hattie realized that she was seeing a spirit. The child was an angel.

Right next to her ear a voice clear as a bell had said, "That is Sam. He is known as the Spirit of Innocence."

Sam was the same age Jamie was now. He was like her spiritual counterpart with some very key differences. Sam would forever remain nine years old, but he was in training to become the youngest, wisest angel ever.

As Hattie watched, Sam had pulled that raggedy blanket up over Jamie to keep her warm. When he touched it, it had turned pure white before returning to its tattered, pink state.

Cynthia, who lay on the couch next to the baby in the basket, never stirred. She slumbered in the deep sleep, unaware of her surroundings, and of anything spiritual going on.

From that time on, Hattie had known Jamie was special. And from that time on, she had seen Sam hovering around Jamie as she grew.

Hattie also knew that Sam didn't realize that sometimes she could see him. Just as she had seen him sitting on the tree branch outside of her window the other day while she was teaching her favorite girl-child about the Lord.

She had learned that he was protective with Jamie, and was most likely eavesdropping to see if she had gotten her teachings right.

She smiled in remembrance. But now the time of the birth of Christ was nearing, and Hattie knew that each year his spirit came to give, not to receive just as he did when he walked the earth as a man.

Praise him!

She had been praising the name of Jesus Christ, since she was a barefoot child running down by the old creek in the Deep South.

On this particular night she found that Jesus was still in the giving business.

She witnessed the Spirit of Innocence touch Jamie's hand. In the course of things the child's hand turned pure red. Hattie knew it was a turning point.

9

The Child and the Devil

Lizzie stood in the Hartford train station, checking train schedules for an upcoming New Year's trip to her sister's house in the Bronx. She was excited about the trip since she hadn't seen her sister in nearly three years. Plus, George had bought her new suits and jewelry to wear during her visit.

As she scanned the schedule searching for the best departure time, Jamie jumped up and down beside her, tugging on her coat. "Grandma Lizzie, I've got to go to the bathroom. Can I? Can I?"

Lizzie hesitated, not wanting her to go alone, but desiring to finish her decision and purchase her ticket.

"Grandma Lizzie, it's only right there." Jamie pointed. And she was right. Lizzie could see the corridor that led to the restroom, just in front of the security guard's station.

She looked over. The old guard smiled. She pointed to Jamie, mouthing the word, "bathroom."

The guard nodded.

"Okay. But you go and come straight back to this spot. No dawdling."

"Okay, Grandma Lizzie," Jamie chirped.

Jamie skipped off to the bathroom. Lizzie shook her head, wondering if that child ever walked anywhere. Even in the house she skipped from room to room. Lizzie would tell her to stop, and for a time that worked, and then she'd be back to skipping again.

Just as Jamie was about to enter the restroom, she heard a man's voice call out to her from the dark recess of the corridor. His words rippled with anger. "Hey little girl."

Jamie turned to see a man who looked as old as a Medusa stone. His skin hung in folds from his skinny frame, and he was dressed in layers upon layers of raggedy clothes. His piercing eyes were fixed on Jamie in pure malice.

Jamie shrank back from the shock of his presence. She wasn't supposed to talk to strangers, so she didn't answer. She just looked at him.

A light sprung from the depths of her eyes causing the man to momentarily shield his eyes. Intent on his purpose, he forged ahead. Laughing, he said, "You're one of those Jesus believers, ain't you?"

With those words he stripped away Jamie's protective armor of not speaking to strangers. She drew herself up to her full height, proud of her newfound knowledge. Smiling, she said, "I am. But how did you know?"

It was his turn to smile now. "Well . . . why don't we just say that Jesus and I sometimes travel the same roads. Therefore we know some of the same people."

Jamie considered this, then said, "I think your road is quite different from the road Jesus travels."

He squinted his eyes in anger. He wanted to strike this smart-mouthed child, but knew he couldn't touch her, at least not yet.

At that moment, a girl, who appeared to be eleven, came racing toward the restroom. She stopped as though startled by something, then she coughed.

The coughing racked her body relentlessly and she couldn't catch her breath.

The man watched the girl steadily. He wondered what Jamie's reaction would be when this girl fell at her feet in the corridor. But before this could be accomplished, Jamie shook her head.

She reached out a hand to the girl and covered the girl's mouth with her other hand. Instantly, the coughing stopped. The girl's breathing returned to normal.

"Thank you," the girl said to Jamie.

Jamie smiled brightly. "The bathroom's right there." The girl went in.

Jamie realized she no longer needed to go to the bathroom. As she headed back to Grandma Lizzie, the man called again, "Hey little girl."

Jamie turned around.

"If you think what you did is such a neat trick, then why don't you slash your wrist with this and see if that little trick will work on you?" He held out a razor blade to her.

Jamie only smiled.

She never knew where the words came from but she said, "Thou shalt not tempt the Lord Thy God. But you know that. Don't you?"

She walked away.

The old man's steady gaze never wavered as Jamie made her way back to her grandmother.

The following morning they found the body of the man in rags, frozen to death on the bus bench outside the terminal. The temperature had dropped that night to below zero and he could not find shelter.

The eleven-year-old girl, who had been on her way to Boston, told her friends about what happened to her at Hartford's train station. Her friends listened patiently but not one of them believed her. For her part she knew she would never forget that little girl with the big brown almond-shaped eyes.

She had felt the air as well as the life leaving her body when the warmth of Jamie's hand had covered her mouth.

The last thing she remembered about the incident was looking back as she entered the bathroom, to see that the little girl's hand had turned pure red.

When she had come out of the bathroom Jamie was gone.

The Living Souls

Deep beneath Hartford, there existed a labyrinth of tunnels that led to various parts of the city. Only one tunnel led to a special place.

This particular passageway had a seal and only things of the spirit filtered through its wings. It was the polar opposite of a cemetery. Instead of bodies, souls existed there, souls that had a very specific purpose.

Mind you, no human had ever crossed its wings, but if they had, they would have beheld beautiful fountains glistening with the miracle of very special gifts.

Hope, Joy, Love, Forgiveness, and Redemption resided there, deep in the bowels of the city. The living spirit of them had but one goal: placement.

This Christmas everything would be different.

Beneath the cross that provided constant light underneath the city, the Soul that was called

Hope said, "I hope one person realizes they need me this year. All it takes is one, and then I can spread myself around."

The Soul of Hope looked longingly toward the exit. He hadn't been allowed to leave in so long he'd forgotten just how many years it had been.

Joy had hoped someone would need him, too, but in order for him to be released there had to be one person in the city in whose heart joy was sparked in all its pureness. Until that happened he was a captured soul, a soul who could not leave.

Solemnly, Hope said to Joy, "It really looks like people don't want you and me. Hope no longer lives in their hearts. They've given up."

The restless Soul of Forgiveness intervened. "Well, if they knew how to utilize me then surely the two of you would come next. And, Love, well you can forget him. They think he's passé."

They all turned to look at the Soul of Love, who was in eternal sleep.

Redemption sighed. His essence soul shivered. "This is all for naught. We're never going to get out of here unless Holiness is unburied."

On the street above them, in the heart of downtown in front of the Old State Building, the Christmas carolers began to sing.

Jamie Lynne stared at the carolers in awe, miming the words to "Silent Night, Holy Night."

Just then, a woman walked past Jamie with a tall candle, the wick of which was unlit. As Jamie turned to look at it, the wick flickered to life. The flame leapt in the air, burning high.

Not one person saw the hand that lit it.

Truly, it was a silent night.

In the silence of this night only one voice would be heard. That voice reigned from a little town called Bethlehem, long, long ago. The sheer power of it would transcend time, just as it always had.

On this night it spoke directly into the heart of one little girl.

It was written, *and a little child shall lead them.*

11

The Brooks Family

Jamie awoke to the delicious smells of cinnamon- and nutmeg-sprinkled French toast, frying bacon, and the boisterous sounds of family, who had arrived for their annual pre-Christmas breakfast.

It was a family tradition.

Every year on a morning before Christmas, and on Christmas Eve, George's sister and her entire brood arrived at his home for the holiday festivities. And what a brood they were.

Jamie jumped out of bed, eager to get to the breakfast table. After washing her face and brushing her teeth, Jamie padded down the stairs.

Lizzie's French toast was a melt-in-your-mouth blend of rich butter, cinnamon, nutmeg, and the warm maple syrup that tasted like it had been freshly tapped from a Vermont tree and warmed.

Christmas was one of the few times a year that

the family put forth an effort to get along and act like *family.*

Jamie's grandfather George and his sister Beatrice were about as different as day was from night. Beatrice was short, heavy, light-skinned, and loud-mouthed with red splotches on her face from too many nights of heavy drinking.

George was tall, slim, dark-skinned, and quiet. And he'd never touched a drop of alcohol in his life, although he kept a fully stocked bar in his house to entertain his guests.

Beatrice was as loud and ghetto as George was quiet and conservative. When she drank, she grew louder and bolder, and more often than not, acid spewed from her tongue.

Despite their differences, she loved her brother. Truly. He was the stable part of the family. The ruling patriarch, so to speak, and he had seen Beatrice's family through some real tough scrapes, financially and otherwise.

Then, of course, there were Beatrice's children, each as different as the man who'd fathered them.

George, on the other hand, had one wife to whom he was loyal and dedicated. He had fathered one child with his wife, and he had one grandchild. He liked stability. The Lord had seen to give him one woman, and he was happy with his Lizzie. Always had been, always would be. What God had put together let no man put asunder.

Hattie sometimes wondered how she could have possibly had two children who were so very different, yet born of the same seed. George and Beatrice both had the same daddy.

And Beatrice's children, truthfully speaking, Hattie on occasion silently considered them demon spawn, though she'd never utter those words aloud about her own flesh and blood grandchildren.

Sharese was the only exception in her mind, and sometimes she could still be the devil in Gucci. Sharese had graduated from Spelman with a 4.0 average, and was the youngest and only black female to hold down the chief financial officer position in a top insurance company.

The fact that the city of Hartford was known worldwide as the Insurance Capital of the World only lent an additional air of prestige to this position.

As a child, Sharese had been a whiz with numbers and still was. Her mind was sharp, photographic, and on point. She was unmarried, so she still carried the family name of Brooks.

Beatrice had never married either of her babies' daddys, and so her children carried the Brooks name. She had five children in all. Her family was well-known in Hartford, thanks mostly to Beatrice's children.

Sharese was a head turner. Sleek, quiet, elegant, with flawless skin the color of dark, rich chocolate. Plus she was smart as a whip and politically and socially connected.

She loved her family and she absolutely adored her young cousin Jamie, who was the reason she was carrying a very exclusive children's bag to her uncle's house, with all types of little girl treasures in it.

Dwayne Brooks, age twenty-four. He was tall, six feet three to be exact, and light-skinned like his mother. He had a slim aristocratic nose, and flashing hazel eyes that a woman could drown in. He was built as though a football field had been designed just to hold him. Dwayne was the type of man who entered a room and stopped conversations. He had deeply dimpled cheeks, curly hair, and a smile that could melt ice cubes. His one drawback was his moodiness. Dwayne was moody to the point of sulkiness at times.

After Jamie's face had been covered with kisses by Sharese and her cheeks pinched by Auntie Beatrice, it was Dwayne's turn to toss her in the air, and land her on the floor in a fit of giggles. Although she was nine years old, Dwayne had been tossing her in the air since she was a baby.

He loved Jamie Lynne, and he never failed to tell her so. He knelt before her, "You're my special girl, Jamie Lynne. You know that, don't you?"

Jamie planted a kiss on Dwayne's brow. She pulled away to look at him as though she could see all his secrets, then she jetted into the kitchen where the rest of the Brooks clan was chattering away.

From the corner of her eye she saw Sharese place the beautiful bag she'd brought for her under the Christmas tree. A single thought sprung to her mind. *I wish Sharese had enough magic to pull my mommy from that bag.*

But suddenly she knew she didn't need to worry because Jesus was going to bring her Mommy home.

All she had to do was believe.

She heard her grandmother's words. "No matter what it looks like Jamie, or how hard it gets, you must believe."

A new string of words were added to her thoughts that didn't come from her grandmother. "Believe Jesus, baby. Believe Jesus." She turned to look to see from whom the words had come. There was no one there.

All she saw was some of her family gathered around the Christmas tree. The lights on the tree twinkled as though they held a secret. The gold star at the top of the tree stood solemnly.

Almost as if she were magnetized, Jamie's eyes watched some of her family members as though she were outside of her body. As quickly as the feeling came, it left.

All that was left was the soft whisper of the words, "Believe Jesus, baby. Believe Jesus."

12

One Child's Love

The rest of the Brooks clan on Beatrice's side was out in full force in the kitchen.

When Jamie entered the kitchen Beatrice's twins, George and Georgette, turned as one to look at her.

They were George's namesake, courtesy of Beatrice. They were also an additional link to George's bank account, or so Beatrice hoped.

The most striking thing about the twins were their deep hued gray eyes with tinges of purple, set in skin the color of caramel. Their eyes had the amazing ability to change colors when they were in a dark mood.

Each was tall and lean. They were athletic types, who looked as though they trained on the track, though nothing could be further from the truth.

George and Georgette reached for Jamie at

the same time. "I saw her first," they said simultaneously as they each knelt and grabbed one of Jamie's arms.

They all burst out laughing, and Jamie hugged Georgette first, and then threw her arms around George's neck. George put a finger under her chin, kissing her on the nose.

He offered her a piece of the bacon he was holding.

Jamie shook her head politely, "No, thank you, George."

"Suit yourself," he shrugged. He went back to his bacon. Lizzie was supplying him with the bacon, fresh from her cast-iron frying pan. Georgette turned up her nose at the smell of pork cooking as she flounced from the kitchen to join her siblings in the living room. George sauntered behind her, still chewing.

Still in the kitchen Jamie turned to her cousin, David, who preferred to be called G-Tang. He refused to answer to anything else.

At seventeen, G-Tang was Beatrice's baby. The entire family doted on him and as was to be expected, he was spoiled rotten. Consequently, he was brought up thinking the world revolved around him. It was quite devastating when he discovered otherwise.

G-Tang's daddy had been the love of Beatrice's life. The man was as fine as the day was long. G-Tang had inherited his extraordinary looks.

He stood six feet one. His eyes were a light topaz framed by long deep chocolate brown lashes that were fringed with a tinge of honey blond.

Even Fashion Fair, with its jars and wands of magic, would have had trouble creating G-Tang's lashes on a woman.

He sported one deeply dimpled cheek, with a cleft in his chin that only lent an air of mystique to his natural handsomeness.

G-Tang also possessed a sulking attitude. He had a way of looking up from under his eyelashes that made most people stop in assessment of themselves. There was nothing deep about this gesture on his part. It was merely a ploy that he used to evaluate people.

Beatrice had loved his daddy so hard and passionately that she had wound up with an exact replica of him in G-Tang. Unfortunately physicality wasn't where the resemblance ended.

Just like his father G-Tang had an internal emotional streak a mile long. He couldn't take pressure and preferred escapism through drugs to realism. This particular trait had landed his father in the federal penitentiary.

Chance Barlow, G-Tang's daddy, was doing life on drug trafficking charges. He was a three-time loser and considered a career criminal. When he was on the streets people used to tease him about his many chances in the game, because of his name, and inevitably one day his chances dried up.

This was much to the chagrin of Old Man Barlow, who owned and lived in a piece of property on the same street as George's home, and was Chance's Daddy and G-Tang's granddaddy. The extraordinary lineage of looks had been inherited from Old Man Barlow's wife, who had since passed on.

G-Tang was a brooder just like Chance. He brooded constantly about school, his family, and the state of the world. He no longer went to school, except for the occasional appearance when Beatrice threatened him.

Instead he preferred spending his time paging for crack. The tips of his fingers were turning black, and had been burnt many times from so much smoking.

Jamie who was standing in front of him now received his famous sullen look. "So what do you want?"

Jamie smiled gently at him. "Nothing, G-Tang."

"So why you standing there then?" he asked harshly.

Lizzie turned to him, giving him a warning look. She needn't have. Jamie could hold her own.

Jamie returned his look. "I'm just standing here, cuz I love you, G-Tang," she whispered softly.

G-Tang averted his eyes, wishing he had a blunt. As soon as breakfast was over, he was going to slip out the back door to the avenue to cop one.

He hadn't wanted to be here anyway.

Beatrice had threatened to throw him out of the house if he were missing in action, and since she babied him, fed him, clothed him in the latest gear, and housed him, as well as kept his pockets phat with paper, despite his drug use, he knew he'd better comply, and comply without a lot of mouth.

G-Tang felt water stinging his eyes. *Now where had that come from?* He hated Jamie. She was so, so, . . . hell, he didn't know, she was just so *something*, and it got on his nerves.

He risked an under-the-velvet-lash glance.

Of course she hadn't moved. She was still standing there. He knew it anyway because he could feel the heat of her presence. Which was another thing that disturbed him about her. For such a little girl, she had a big presence.

Jamie watched him steadily.

She stuck out her hand. She touched a gentle fingertip to the corner of G-Tang's eye, as though she could see the invisible tears. The touch was featherlight, yet it felt as if a multitude of hands had touched him.

Jamie cocked her head staring directly into the inner beauty of his eyes, looking beyond the addiction, the sullenness, and the crack.

"I love you, G-Tang," she said once again softly.

G-Tang welled up inside. No longer able to sit in his chair comfortably, he pulled in his sprawling legs. He got up to head for the bathroom. "Excuse me."

Jamie stepped to the side.

Lizzie didn't even turn around from honey buttering her biscuits this time. It was the Christmas season, a time for miracles.

In the bathroom G-Tang sat on the edge of the tub, after bolting the door. He broke down in tears.

In the kitchen Jamie said, "Grandma Lizzie, can I have a biscuit with some jelly?"

"You sure can, baby." Lizzie put some jelly on a warm honey buttered biscuit, handing it to Jamie.

Jamie took a bite, closed her eyes at the deliciousness, and smiled.

13

The Spirit and the Past

Sam smiled at the exact instant as Jamie, albeit he smiled some three hundred-plus years in the past, where he was residing for the time being. Sam and the Spirit of Discernment were observing Jamie's slavery lineage, as well as the customs of the slaves celebrating Christmas in the past.

Discernment watched Sam's delighted reactions as he watched the slaves shucking corn and singing during Christmas. Sam didn't realize that a lot of the joy was due more to the fact that the slaves had their only respite from their back-breaking labor, rather than to the celebration of the birth of the Christ Child. As the singing continued the smile began to vanish from Sam's face, as he slowly realized something vital was missing. Suddenly the scene before him darkened, as though someone had dimmed the lights.

He turned to Discernment, anxiety etched into his young features. He jumped up and down in distress.

"They don't know Jesus," he said.

Discernment folded his arms. "What makes you say that?"

Sam's eyes widened in astonishment at Discernment's question. He sighed loudly.

Discernment pretended not to notice Sam's growing distress.

"They haven't once said his name," Sam screeched. "Say his name! Say his name! Say his name!"

The corn shucking and singing grew louder, though not one of the slaves ever uttered the name of Jesus.

Discernment sighed softly. "Their masters have plied them with alcohol, and a taste of freedom for the day, and so this is more of a break from work for them than a celebration of Christ's birth."

Sam studied the scene unhappily, and mumbled, "I don't see how Jamie Lynne came from this lineage. We're going to have to step up her teaching. She has genes inside her that could be dead to the Christ Child." Sam kicked at the dirt with the toe of his shoe.

Discernment smiled. "She's been given all that she needs. Besides, not all is lost Sam. In 1707 Isaac Watts published hymns and spiritual songs. They were a salve to the spirit of the slaves. In 1779 the Second Great Awakening began with the Cane Ridge Camp meeting. The meeting took place in Kentucky and embraced African

Americans. Many of the slaves converted to Christianity."

Discernment now had Sam's full attention. "In 1800, the state of Virginia passed a law forbidding African Americans to assemble between sunset and sunrise for religious worship or for instruction. But as I mentioned, little one, all was not lost."

Sam studied Discernment intently now. He had calmed his jumping to a simple shifting from one foot to the other.

"Look there." Discernment pointed.

As he did so, they were transported to a place deep in the Virginia woods. A Black woman of indeterminate age was sitting with her head bowed and legs crossed in a small clearing with twigs burning and flames shooting up at her feet.

The stars in the sky twinkled down on her. The stars were so bright they lit the area she was sitting in. It looked like silver twilight shone upon the earth.

On a tree branch directly above her head sat a bald eagle, as commanding as a general in the army. The area surrounding the woman was hushed.

Sam was about to speak when the woman lifted her head to stare straight at them. Sam gasped at the sight of her. Her entire face was bathed in white luminescent light. She didn't possess any features. But you could feel the power of the eyes that you couldn't see watching you. Her entire face was an oval of light.

"Who's she?" Sam asked in awe.

"She *is* the Spirit of Worship. She has always been here and she will always be here, until she is no longer needed. When the slaves were forbidden to worship the Lord, she worshipped for them, in their place. Our God is a mighty God, Sam. No human has ever stepped foot on this spot of land. No human ever will."

Sam's eyes widened and a chill ran through him at Discernment's words.

"This clearing is in a realm not known to man," Discernment continued. "She is a Spiritual Stand-In. The grace of Christ has once again kept all from being lost."

At that precise moment the woman threw her head back and sang the most beautiful song. The woman sang a hymn, "The Call."

> *Oh can't you hear*
> *the Lord calling*
> *his voice both then*
> *and now.*
>
> *The Lord is calling*
> *the Lord is calling*
> *How bittersweet is*
> *his sound.*
>
> *When all is lost*
> *his trumpet sounds*
> *the souls that are*
> *lost, are found.*
>
> *Oh Precious Lord*
> *Oh Precious Lord*

*I know I hear
your call. Now I
can't fall. Now I
stand tall, to declare
your name to all.*

*I hear his voice
I have no choice
I go unburdened
and unbound.*

*Your name to all
Your name to all
with you, I shall
not fall.*

*Now I stand tall
so does your name,
to all, with you I
shall not fall.*

*The Lord is calling
the Lord is calling
How bittersweet is
his sound.*

*I hear his voice
I have no choice
I go unburdened
and unbound.*

Just when Sam thought she was finished, she switched songs. She continued on, her voice soft and powerful. The song was, "Say His Name."

When she stopped singing, the hush returned. It was startling in contrast to the heartfelt singing. She opened her arms wide in a position of worship, then she stood. The stars descended as though to embrace her. Then she assumed the highest level of worship as she bent to her knees.

She bowed her head.

The light from her face was doused low. Sam let out a breath that he hadn't realized he was holding. "Say his name, Jesus! Say his name, Jesus!" Sam sang softly the words ringing in his ears.

Discernment stared at the bald eagle that returned his stare, and never moved. "Jamie Lynne Brooks will receive a special gift tonight, Sam. She will receive the gift of worship," Discernment said.

It was actually daytime where Jamie was standing but the Spirit of Worship would reach up from the night to touch her.

As Discernment spoke, Sam saw Jamie bite into a jellied biscuit.

The Spirit of Worship rose from her knees and reached out a hand. It spanned the years and distance to touch the girl-child, Jamie, lightly on the crown of her head.

Jamie looked up briefly, as though she could see the Spirit. Then she took another bite of her biscuit, heading for the dining room where the family breakfast was about to take place.

The Spirit of Worship returned to her sitting position.

Sam and Discernment took a last look at the crystal twilight surrounding the ageless black woman. Their ears prickled and the hairs stood up on the back of their necks from the depth of the silence and solitude.

"It's amazing," Sam said.

"Amazing Grace," Discernment agreed.

14

The Pre-Christmas Breakfast

Sam stumbled into the dining room, catching his balance next to the dining room table that Jamie was putting the finishing touches on. Jamie was intent on making sure everything was in its proper place. Her grandmother's table was as stylish as any from a holiday cookbook.

Discernment shook his head at Sam's stumbling, as he was reminded once again that Sam still didn't have quite a grasp on gravity in this realm.

"Perhaps one day," he mumbled under his breath.

Just as he was going to ask if Sam wanted to be seated near the food on the buffet where there were two stools, Sam said, "Let's sit there."

Sam brushed off his pants legs. He headed for a stool, wondering what that honey buttered jelly biscuit Jamie was still munching on tasted like.

As an angel, Sam required no food, water, or substance of any kind. Only when he had to cross the realms and appear as an earthly body did he require those things. And only then did he taste food, or experience certain human elements, and even then it was only in the rarest of instances.

Lately he'd been experiencing the human side a bit more. Sam knew what it was like to be hot and cold. And what it felt like to fall down and skin his knees.

He conjured up the memories from his earthly experiences the aromas from food, such as the ones coming from Lizzie's kitchen. He smiled fondly as he remembered the taste of food. He watched Jamie stuff the last of the giant biscuit into her mouth.

"Come on." Discernment tugged on his sleeve. Sam could be such a child sometimes.

Sam reluctantly turned away, scrambling toward the stool.

"I want to be seated when George arrives with Hattie. This is quite an assembly of family that you're going to see here today," the Spirit of Discernment said.

"They're really ordinary compared to Jamie," Sam observed.

"That is precisely why she is needed, young one." Discernment settled his robes around him. Although his primary assignments were in contemporary times, he never varied his clothing. As an Elder angel, his robes were always pristine, and impeccably kept in place.

His robes served as a reminder of how differently things operated in the spirit. It was another world from what people knew. There also wasn't any day or night in the spiritual world they inhabited.

Only the Spirit of the Lord lighted their world.

Just then George walked in with Hattie beside him. She was walking with what she called her dress-up cane. Hattie was done up from head to toe in gold. She sparkled just like the angels on Lizzie's tree. A spot of ruby red rouge dotted her cheeks.

Hattie's eyes sparkled mischievously as she looked ahead to what she considered to be the breakfast of the year.

Upon her entry, a chorus of "Good morning, Grandma," greeted her.

Instantly Dwayne and Sharese were at her side. Dwayne removed her coat. Sharese bestowed a warm hug on her.

Hattie's bejeweled hand carrying her oldest ruby ring, and stunning gold 24-carat triplicate layered wedding band, touched Sharese's smooth dark chocolate cheek.

Beatrice nodded from her seat.

George and Georgette each bestowed a kiss, one on each cheek. Of course it was Jamie who broke through the formality and fanfare. She flew into Hattie's arms, embracing her as though she were the most important person in the world. "Hi, Grandma. Welcome to breakfast!"

Hattie closed her eyes as she wrapped her arms around Jamie. Just as quickly as she had come, Jamie left, sprinting back to the kitchen to help Grandma Lizzie. She was the second chef in command, and she was in charge of last-minute details of the meal.

Immediately feeling the void of Jamie's absence, Hattie looked around, noticing G-Tang was missing. Hattie didn't appreciate the chain of respect being broken. Lizzie was the only exception since she was the chef, and really only an in-law. She wasn't blood.

As she walked imperiously with her head in the air, she inquired of Beatrice with a bit of a sting to her voice. "Where's David?"

Sam chuckled at Hattie's airs.

Discernment shot him a glance that wiped the smile from his face. Sam enjoyed the old woman's antics. He thought she was feisty.

Beatrice waved her hand airily at her mother. "I don't know. He's around here somewhere."

As if on cue, G-Tang emerged from the bathroom. He was glad not to see Jamie. But his grandmother not yet seated was a close second to Jamie. She stood there, imperially staring at him as though waiting for him to bow.

G-Tang knew this was not going to be his day. He hated Christmas with a passion. He wished he could wipe Christmas from the calendar. Every year it was the same old garbage. He was so sick of it. He didn't do family well, and every Christmas they made a big to-do out of these family traditions.

First Jamie and now this, G-Tang lamented.

His mother was always forcing him to do stuff, controlling and wielding her purse strings over his head. He saw Beatrice smile slyly knowing what was coming his way.

"David." His grandmother's voice cracked like a whip.

Beatrice loved it when her mother berated her beautiful, stank-attitude son.

G-Tang squared his shoulders and rushed over to his grandmother. He kissed her lightly on the forehead, and then made sure her pillow was situated just as she liked it before he assisted her in sitting.

She was the only person in the world completely immune to the fine specimen of beauty he exuded, or so he thought.

Hattie stared at him, sensing an inner turmoil as well as a shift in emotions in him. She watched him intently, and then decided against calling him out. Instead she said, "So how are you, David?"

"I'm fine, Grandma. And you?"

Hattie sniffed. "I'm always well, boy. You know that." David lifted her bejeweled hand to his lips, kissing it. She peered at him from under her lashes, a trait very much like his own.

"Can I get you a glass of orange juice, Grandma?"

Hattie preened. Secretly she had a bit of a soft spot for David when he wasn't in demonic mode chasing drugs. She was well aware of what he did. He was just like his father.

"Yes, son. That would be nice," Hattie responded, deciding to let him off the hook. The twins snickered until a withering glance from Hattie was cast their way. G-Tang rolled his eyes at them.

"I'd like a glass of orange juice, too, David," Beatrice stated mockingly, enjoying herself at G-Tang's expense.

G-Tang only nodded, deciding next time she woke up looking for that bottle of J&B, its contents would be in the toilet.

Glad to escape, he headed for the kitchen. Jamie smiled as she passed him on her way to the dining room.

"So Muh-Dear," Beatrice said using the old Southern term for Mother Dear. "You're looking well today."

Hattie positioned her head so as to be able to get a better look at Beatrice. Noting the splotchiness on her cheeks and the puffed eyes that the pancake makeup wasn't hiding, she wished she could say the same. But she wasn't about to fix her lips to tell a bald-faced lie. Instead she merely responded, "Thank you, Beatrice."

Beatrice rolled her eyes as though she could read her mother's mind.

George lit his pipe while settling in his chair, observing the years-old friction between his mother and sister.

Beatrice turned to him, trying to blow off some of the heat Hattie always managed to stir up in her. Now that her focus wasn't on David, Beatrice felt stripped naked by her mother's probing eyes. She'd told everyone who'd listen that her mother was harmless, that her bark was worse than her bite, and she didn't believe one word of it. Beatrice had a reputation for being tough, and the fact that she had been, and still was, afraid of her own mother, would only taint her reputation.

Many of the street brawls Beatrice had won had been due to her anger at her mother and her need of a whipping post in which to take it out on.

Watching her brother puff contentedly on his pipe, Beatrice decided he was an easier target. "George, why you smoking that pipe before breakfast? You know that smoke will float into the food."

George laid his pipe in the ashtray, not rising to Beatrice's bait. "Uh huh," he said. He watched his twin namesakes take seats at the backgammon and checker board table. He wondered why they bothered because every year they get worked up about who was better, as well as who had cheated.

Hattie's focus remained on Beatrice. "If that's the only habit George has, then I thank the Lord for that," Hattie stated, her voice laced with a double meaning.

The tension became quite thick.

Beatrice was steaming. Hattie always took up for George, no matter what. Beatrice bit the inside of her cheek, a habit she'd developed as a child when her mother angered her. "David!" she called. "Where's that juice?"

Sam put his chin in his hand. "Why is she afraid of her mother? She's a grown woman."

Discernment laughed. "Because Hattie has a second pair of eyes, given to her by the Lord."

Sam's own eyes widened as a possibility occurred to him that he had never considered. "Do you think she can see us?"

Before the Spirit of Discernment could answer, Hattie winked, in the direction of the buffet.

Sam fell off his stool. He stumbled as he tried to get up from the floor.

Discernment stated quietly, as though Sam were still sitting calmly next to him, "She has been given the sight to protect the child. She was born with it many years before Jamie ever entered the world."

In the kitchen, Jamie bowed her head and whispered a Christmas prayer for her family. The instant she finished the prayer, the antique grandfather clock in the living room chimed, indicating it was time for pre-Christmas breakfast to begin.

The striking of the hour was also heard by the stranger poised outside of their front door.

Sam resettled himself on the stool. His spirit stirred. Discernment glanced down on him, and a light shone from his eyes, raining down on Sam, who basked in the glow of it.

"Peace, be still," Sam said softly.

Just then the doorbell rang.

15

Elijah

Beatrice rose from the sofa. "George, who would be ringing the bell this time of the morning? Everyone's already here."

"I don't know, Bee," he said. "But it might behoove you to answer the door and see so we can get on with this breakfast."

Beatrice rushed to the door and pulled it open without even looking through the peephole.

Standing before her was a stranger.

The man was rail thin. He stood erect with flashing piercing light brown eyes. His eyes were in stark contrast to his coal black skin, which had a look of chiseled marble.

His clothes, clearly a bit tattered as well as old, were clean. They were also neatly pressed. The man wore the clothes with a great deal of pride. His bearing was one of great humbleness, although one could sense great power.

Beatrice's acid tongue was about to spew out, "Who are you?" But for some reason her tongue was stuck to the roof of her mouth, and all she could do was stare at this man with his commanding presence.

She blinked. Finally she opened her mouth, but nothing came out. Opening her mouth was the only form of physical expression she seemed capable of.

Upstairs, Sam and Discernment exchanged looks.

The hair on Hattie's arms prickled, and a chill raced through her body. Her eyes wide, she envisioned a man from another time at a woman's door asking to be fed. A host of black birds were circling the woman's house.

Just as Jamie passed Hattie as though a force were leading her downstairs, Hattie said, "Baby, invite the man in for breakfast."

Jamie gave a small smile.

"And tell Auntie Beatrice to come upstairs." She wanted to add, "And, tell her to close her mouth, too," but she refrained. Though she was upstairs, she could see Beatrice gaping at the man.

George, who normally would not have allowed a stranger to cross his threshold, took his cue from his mother. He didn't cotton to messing with things he didn't know about. So he simply called out, "Lizzie, set another place at the table. We're having company."

In the kitchen, Lizzie looked at the wall clock that had stopped ticking. It was frozen in time. A shiver ran through her body at George's words.

"Okay, sweetheart. I'll bring another setting right out," she said, not even questioning George's on-the-spot addition.

Dwayne and Sharese exchanged glances but that was all.

The twins got up from the checker game. They huddled together on the couch, their eyes now fastened for some reason on the staircase.

G-Tang, who was once again sitting with his legs sprawled out in front of him, gauged the total shift in temperature in the room. He thought, *Lord I wish I had a blunt.*

A response blew right through him. *You don't need a blunt, David.* Someone was breathing right next to his ear. He turned his head but no one was there. G-Tang sat up, fear tingling through his every limb. His skin had turned clammy.

Jamie finally reached the bottom step. They all watched silently as only Beatrice came up the stairs, looking as though ten years had been shaved from her life.

Hattie's heart thumped at the sight of her.

At the bottom of the stairs Jamie smiled brightly. She stuck out her hand. "Hi, I'm Jamie Lynne Brooks," she said formally.

The man at the door returned Jamie's smile. "I know who you are, Jamie. Merry Christmas."

Jamie's eyes widened. "You do?"

"Yes."

"How do you know me?"

Lowering his voice to a whisper, he bent down to her level, and asked, "Can you keep a secret?"

Jamie nodded vigorously.

"I know you because we're related. Though not in flesh."

Jamie stood with her small hand in his grip as though it were the most natural thing in the world, feeling the truth of his words.

"You're here for breakfast, right?"

"Right."

"Come in. Welcome to our home. Let me hang up your coat."

He handed his coat to her. The tattered old coat looked out of place on the sparkling cherry wood coat rack.

Jamie reached out and hand in hand they ascended the staircase.

"Let me introduce you to my family," she said. "What's your name?"

"Elijah," the man responded. "My name is Elijah."

"Do you have a last name?" Jamie inquired. She'd never met anyone who didn't have a last name.

"Elijah's all I need," the man responded.

Jamie's eyes glowed with a special light. She smiled. She turned on the step for an instant and threw her arms impulsively around the stranger's neck.

Touched deep in his spirit the stranger hugged the little girl back. And that was how a spirit many years old came to breakfast one pre-Christmas morning in the hood.

Outside of George's house a sea of black-birds surrounded it, lining up in the formation of a battalion. They were on the roof, in the front yard, as well as in the backyard.

They covered practically every inch of space available. When the stranger departed so would they.

"My name is Elijah," the stranger whispered once again.

The Elijah Spirit

As Elijah stepped into the foyer of George's house, the grandfather clock stopped ticking. So did the timepiece around George's neck, though he had yet to notice it.

Everything in the house came to a brief standstill for that moment, though the Brooks family would never realize it. The only animation of life in that instance was the two angels who were present in spirit, and of course Elijah.

Sam opened his mouth to speak, found he couldn't, nor could he sense any unasked questions, so instead he got off the stool. Not once did he stumble as he bowed down in a form of worship.

Elijah's voice was soft but deep. "Get up little one. You and I are much alike."

The little child angel rose as he'd been instructed to. He had to shield his eyes from the great and powerful light emanating from Elijah's eyes.

The Spirit of Discernment rose, his robes swishing around him.

Elijah waved his hand, moved closer, and embraced the age-old spirit. Discernment felt eternal peace blow from Elijah. He embraced Elijah as though he never wanted to let go.

Elijah finally stepped back from the embrace. He surveyed the room, smiling. He ventured over to George, who was sitting in his favorite seat.

Elijah put a hand to George's chest. His hand became white as he healed the illness in George's body. A couple of seconds passed, and his hand returned to its normal coal black coloring.

He then smiled down at Jamie, who was frozen in her stance of looking up at him.

Elijah nodded to the two angels, and took the plate of food that had been prepared for him. For some reason Lizzie had already filled the plate with food.

Elijah descended the staircase as silently as he had come. He retrieved his old worn and tattered coat along the way. The coat had survived many centuries.

When he stepped onto the front porch, the blackbirds assembled in formation. Then they flew away.

Sam let out a breath he didn't know he'd been holding. So did Discernment.

In a trembling voice, Sam asked, "What did he just do?"

Discernment gazed out the window, watching the blackbirds fly away in perfect formation. "Jamie's grandfather had lung cancer. The lung cancer was spreading throughout his body. He hadn't told the family. No need now. He doesn't have it anymore, which he'll soon discover."

Later, each family member would examine the memory as though it were a dream. And until the day she died, Lizzie would always wonder what happened to her extra gold and ivory place setting.

The clocks began to tick again, all except the timepiece George wore around his neck. It would remain frozen in time, never to tick again.

The family continued to breakfast, basking in the peace left behind as well as enjoying one another's company, more sincerely than they had in a long time.

The conversation Jamie and the stranger had replayed itself in spirit, like a taped recording echoing throughout the realms.

"What's your name?"

"Elijah," the man responded. "My name is Elijah."

"Do you have a last name," Jamie inquired.

"Elijah's all I need," the man had responded. Elijah.

On a clear brisk, cold morning he arrived at one family's pre-Christmas breakfast. The pattern for the gift of miracles had been established.

17

The First Miracle

George stepped out into the briskly cold day in front of the Collin Bennett Building.

He pulled his cashmere scarf a bit tighter around his neck, the way his Lizzie had taught him, to ward against the chill of the day. Though that chill was nothing compared to the one that was still running through his body at his doctor's words. The power of which were stuck in his mind like when people played a record in his day, and the needle got stuck in a groove.

"George," the doctor had said with nothing less than astonishment, laced with disbelief in his voice.

"George," he repeated as though he'd never called George's name the first time. "There's no trace of cancer." His voice had dropped to the lowest of whispers.

George had to strain to hear him. "George, it's gone. The cancer is gone. There isn't a trace of it." The doctor's voice ended in a note of total dismay, laced with something akin to awe, as he studied the X-rays before him.

They were the same X-rays that had spelled death for the man sitting in his office the last time he'd looked at them.

Impossible.

The doctor shook his head.

Impossible.

Both the old X-rays, as well as the new set he had ordered, were clear of cancer, and he knew for a fact the old ones had displayed the cancer with vivid clarity, sounding a death knell for the man sitting in his office.

Consequently George's entire day had been filled with a rush as well as with a battery of medical tests and re-exams by Hartford's brightest in the field of medicine.

At the end of the day the final conclusion remained the same.

The brightest brains in medicine had concurred. Many of the doctors had cleared their jam-packed schedules to participate in the re-exams, due to the unusual circumstances. A cancer had vanished from the old X-rays, and never shown up on the new.

The cancer was gone.

Nary a trace of it was to be found. George Brooks was cancer free. There was no doubt.

George had received the final words of this gift, for the second time that day from his primary physician, which is what found him now standing in front of the Collin Bennett building, tugging at his cashmere scarf trying to decipher exactly what had happened.

All he could recall was a dream he'd had where a rail thin man, with skin the color of dark black coal, and hypnotic light brown eyes, had put a hand to his chest.

And the dream was so fleeting he couldn't even really be sure he'd had it. Maybe he'd imagined it. Or saw a scene from television or something, and it transferred into his sleep.

Lizzie was what he called a "nightaholic" and not being able to sleep, she frequently watched television late into the night. He'd told her many times to turn it off, because that stuff sometimes seeped into his sleep.

Regardless of how this particular circumstance had been conceived he brightened. Now, he'd never have to tell his precious Lizzie, Jamie, and Cynthia the bad news, because he didn't have the cancer anymore. The cancer was indeed gone, which meant he didn't have to leave his precious girls alone.

And he knew for a fact on his own that the cancer was gone, because the cancer had been very invasive. He had felt it throughout his chest and body.

He had been fast approaching more radical treatment, the kind that would have been difficult to hide.

But he knew nonetheless it was gone because his body was reacting to the freedom of it. Come to think of it, he'd felt its absence since the family pre-Christmas breakfast.

George was not a praying man but he decided a prayer of thanks was certainly warranted on this day. And right there in front of God and the Collin Bennett building, with no shame in his game, George Brooks dropped down on bended knee and gave a prayer of thanks to the Lord Jesus Christ.

Before he rose, he decided the streets of Hartford could use a little praying for too. So he extended his prayers to include one for all of the children in the city being killed. As well he prayed for the drug users, drug dealers, gangstas, whores, homeless people, alcoholics, and the like.

Though a few people ventured down the avenue and looked at this man on bended knee on the street strangely, George didn't care. Sometimes a man had to give the Lord his due and his respect, no matter where he was.

In the shadows of the Artist Collective building, generally known as the brainchild of Dottie McLean, and built on the very great talent of her husband, the late jazz musician, Jackie McLean, G-Tang stood in rigid shock watching his very dignified uncle, on his knees in a very expensive pair of sharkskin trousers, on the avenue of all places, praying.

Just then a loud squawking rent the air. A large blackbird with wings at least a foot in diameter flew from the roof of the Artist Collective building.

Across the street George ended his prayer.

He looked at the timepiece around his neck and for the first time he noticed its hands were frozen on a specific set of numbers, as though they were etched in clay. A light that had never before shown on the watch lit the dial. In fact there'd never been a light on the watch.

The hands on the watch would forever mark the time of Elijah's appearance. But, George

Brooks would never know that. He clutched the timepiece to his chest comforted by the warmth generating from it. And, in spite of it all, somehow he knew that it marked a great change in his life.

18

The Round Table

George sipped thoughtfully from his cup of coffee at McDonald's on the avenue. His heart sang its own tune every time he replayed the whispered awe in the doctor's voice. "George, it's gone. The cancer's gone."

A smile lit his face. His eyes shone brightly with unshed tears.

At fifty-eight years of age, George could remember every single incident in his life that had ever produced a tear, but the ones he felt this morning were among the most profound.

McDonald's' central location in the hood made it a hub of activity, as well as the place to be to hear local gossip. It was the gathering place for some of the old heads in the city.

Most of the old heads considered themselves Hartford's voices of wisdom. Most passersby considered the old men annoying, as they picked apart every situation—good, bad, or otherwise—in the city.

These men also considered themselves ministers of the Gospel. Their own brands of gospel in any case.

This day was no different—as usual there was a lively debate going on.

Nearby, Hartford's chess champion Darryl Payne was being challenged by yet another opponent who had sworn by the life of his mother that he would take Darryl's title.

It had yet to happen, and it wouldn't. But each successive challenger sought the same victory.

Darryl lived in a shelter. He carried only a backpack that held his chess set, which he kept polished to a high shine. He wore the same clothes most days, but they were always clean and well kept.

He usually couldn't spring for more than a cup of coffee with the change in his pocket. The money he won from chess bought dinner so he wouldn't have to eat the shelter food, and laundered his clothes. That wasn't all it did but most people weren't privy to that.

Darryl Payne was a simple young man in his early thirties, who'd fallen on hard times and had only one love, chess. He didn't have the capacity to keep a job or earn a living in the tradition of most Americans.

Yet he was a mathematical genius, one of Hartford's brightest minds. This explained why he was about 100 to 0 when it came to chess. And that score was counting only this particular season.

George, who knew most of those present, continued to sip his coffee and observe the chess game. He also kept an ear tuned to the day's topic of conversation being dished out, by the old heads.

George owned a great deal of both residential and commercial real estate in the city, so he knew a great many of the city's residents, as well as most of the business owners. In fact, he had at one time owned the land McDonald's was sitting on. He'd made a pretty penny from its sale.

When the riots of the '70s destroyed the majority of Hartford's Black businesses, George had cut his losses, and invested in real estate.

Hartford's Black neighborhood had never recovered its economic base. It was now a shell torn of the brightness of dreams.

Roaming this area now were some of the worst cases of drug abuse, criminal activity, and lost hopes and dreams in Hartford's history.

George shook his head, pulling himself back to the present and observed Darryl setting up his opponent for the kill. At a nearby table, another potential victim watched, awaiting his chance to challenge Darryl's genius.

George wondered why they bothered, since no one yet had bested Darryl but he imagined it was a thirst for the possibility of winning, and taking down an undefeatable champ in the process. The thought of wearing his crown kept them coming.

George also knew there was more to Darryl than met the eye. Darryl lived in the shelter, and he spent nearly everything he had on his young daughter. He supported her in style, though he lacked most of the essential things for himself. Darryl was a stand-up guy.

George had once offered him a place to stay in one of his buildings at a greatly reduced rate. He'd thanked George profusely, but politely declined. He hadn't wanted to take unnecessary money away from his daughter's care. She was a smart girl at thirteen years of age, intellectually advanced, like her dad.

Darryl intended to give her what he'd never had, and that was a *chance.* George had had nothing but respect for Darryl from that day on.

Darryl intended to remain homeless so he could see his daughter through Yale University. He had $88,000 stashed away that he had been scrimping and winning through chess over many years. His goal was to have his daughter's entire tuition by the time she was ready to start college.

He planned to hand over a certified bank check for the full tuition to Yale University. He still had many dollars to go, which is why he was concentrating and strategizing so hard on his game.

To Darryl, chess was a game of strategy, of winning and losing, of life's education. Once he handed over the check to Yale, he would retire from playing chess.

He would call out his final checkmate.

The old heads watched the game too. They shook their heads as they saw defeat fast approaching Darryl's latest opponent.

One of them turned angrily in his seat to look at another one, from his own table, as he tuned in to what was being said. "Man, shut-up. You don't know nothing about Christmas. You come in here with that ying-yang, pagan Christmas stuff. Let it rest, Bob. I'm telling you let it rest. That ain't truth, and you know it."

"Humph. What the hell do you know?" Bob responded.

"I know Christmas isn't the result of some man in a red suit," Charlie stated heatedly.

Those words set it off. They kicked the day's roundtable into high gear. Approximately fifteen men in the city were part of the old heads and joined the lively discussions.

Seldom were they all there at once and none appeared on weekends. However, daily they took turns being there.

Today there was an eclectic mix. There was a Jehovah's Witness and an Ethiopian Black Jew who was a picture of pride, tradition, and dignity. There was also a Baptist, and two Pentecostals weighing in. That meant the discussion of Christmas and religion was about to get seriously heated, as Bob was now demonstrating.

He had the full attention of the table now, with the mention of Santa Claus.

It was a good thing Paul Mitchell wasn't present because they really would have gotten an earful, since this was a sore spot with him regarding the fairy tale Christmas fed to Black children.

George smiled and took another sip of coffee, awaiting the explosion.

Raymond who was the Ethiopian Black Jew and the one who among them was the most in touch with his heritage and religious traditions, dropped a bomb in the middle of the conversations.

His words hit their target with a ripple effect.

"I don't know how you guys can be so upset about an altered history. I done told you time and time again, there's only one God who guided us through the Old Testament. There's only one set of laws, and those are the Ten Commandments, end of story. If the world was following those laws, it wouldn't be in the state it is now."

Charlie, a devout Pentecostal believer who hadn't attended church in twenty years because he didn't want to contribute to making the ministers rich, said, "Raymond, Jesus Christ is the son of God, and he is the reason for the season of Christmas. If everybody would stop running out and buying all those unnecessary gifts, trying to impress each other, maybe somebody could see it."

Raymond only shook his head. They'd been down this road before. He knew what he knew and that was that. It was a sorry shame that so many Black people didn't know their history, spiritual or otherwise, and most he knew didn't have a clue as to their heritage.

He'd never held much to religious debates anyway. Furious now at Charlie's inability to see any point of view but his own, he clamped his mouth shut. In time he knew life would show them better than he could tell them.

Bob, being the Baptist that he was and feeling there was nothing wrong with the myth of Santa Claus, said, "Charlie, stop force-feeding us. Every man has got to know God for himself. If people like believing in Santa Claus, and if it makes them happy, what harm can it do?"

Darryl looked up from the chess game for

the first time, just before he was about to call checkmate. Normally he didn't participate in the debates with the old heads but that statement riled him.

He spoke quietly yet his words had the effect of a loud trumpet in their midst. "Not knowing the truth can do a lot of harm," Darryl said. Then he looked at his opponent, made his final move, and said, "Checkmate."

He held out his hand for his money and his opponent frowned.

All the old heads looked at him in astonishment. He rarely spoke unless spoken to.

He had silenced them with a single remark.

As Darryl counted his money and the next victim took the seat across from him he looked up for a brief moment and said, "Jesus Christ is real. The day of his birth should be revered and honored."

He stuffed his pocket with the money. Then he reset the chessboard to start a new game.

On that note George rose to leave. Under his breath he uttered, "Amen."

19

G-Tang

G-Tang was in one of his deep funks. He had laced his last blunt liberally with crack cocaine, and he was still having trouble getting mellow.

Jamie had messed his head up so bad. It was as if she had blown all of his future highs. That girl got on his last nerve.

He puffed angrily. He didn't need or want anyone's sympathy. He took out a glassine bag, shoveling cocaine into his nose. Sniffing was a vice from back in the day.

Most of G-Tang's crew smoked crack either through blunts or a pipe. But G-Tang was friends with some of the cats from back in the day, and they had shared the lost art of sniffing cocaine with him. His father, Chance Barlow, was known for having a hole in his nose from sniffing so much cocaine.

The coke burned G-Tang's nostrils as he waited for the desired effect. Yet there was nothing. He couldn't believe it. Here he sat in a dark corner of the attic, sniffing, and smoking simultaneously at that, and he couldn't feel anything.

All he could do was hear Jamie's voice like a broken record. *"I'm just standing here, cuz I love you, G-Tang."* Following that particular annoyance was the vision of Uncle George down on his knees, on the avenue, praying.

If Beatrice had had any inkling of what he was going through, he could just hear her saying, "You'd better stop smoking them damn drugs, David. Maybe, then you'll stop hallucinating."

Hell to the nah.

He wasn't crazy. Yet nobody would believe him if he told them. But he *had* seen his Uncle George, on the avenue on his knees, praying.

On second thought he could have been hallucinating. He'd heard of people tripping like that, after getting some bad drugs. But, deep inside he knew it wasn't so. He'd actually seen his uncle praying.

Why his uncle would be on his knees praying on the avenue was really the question at hand.

He'd seen what he'd seen and that was it.

G-Tang took another couple of sniffs. Nothing. Not even a mild ping. He relit the blunt taking a few more pulls, still nothing. Frustrated, he tapped the blunt out in the ashtray. He rose from his favorite spot in the attic, stretching out his cramped legs.

No one ever went into the attic but him.

He liked to smoke there because there was a window to let the smoke out of the house. Plus it kept him from hearing Beatrice. His time spent in the attic was like going through self-imposed solitary confinement, but he could deal with that, because he could leave, whenever he liked.

The attic was stuffed with treasures, as well as family mementos. There were personal belongings from all of their growing-up years. Yet G-Tang never bothered to look, feel, or notice his surroundings.

He simply went to the attic to drown his blues. Since he was having trouble doing that today he wandered around and for the first time since he'd begun his haunts to the attic, his curiosity was piqued, and he wondered what some of the things were, and what memories they might hold.

One of the lightbulbs flickered, finally staying lit.

G-Tang picked up a dust-covered box. He put it back down without opening it. He didn't like what he'd felt.

Walking over to the window he peered out, paranoid as he thought someone was watching him. It was a ridiculous thought, since the window overlooked the roof, and the only way anyone could be looking through the window is if they were actually standing on the roof.

The hairs on his arms were raised so he checked it out anyway.

He didn't see anyone on the roof but he continued to stare, out into the open space, as if someone might appear.

He stood there for half an hour, staring at the same spot out that window. Though, if you had asked him he'd have said he was only standing there for a few minutes.

He walked the exact path back to the dust-covered box, standing in front of it. Still he didn't touch it. Instead he wandered down another aisle.

Funny enough there seemed to be clear parallel paths to walk through, separated by time.

G-Tang was so tall he had to lower his head to walk through the attic. And at that moment for the first time he realized that the attic was huge. One big wide-open space filled with pieces of their lives, their pasts, and their present.

G-Tang ruminated on how much he hated this time of the year. Christmas was depressing to him. All people did was run around with false smiles, knowing they couldn't stand each other the rest of the year. They faked the funk by buying presents that in his opinion made them feel better than the actual recipient of the gifts.

All he knew was that Christmas was depressing. Every year as it approached he got a heavy feeling, and his heart felt like lead. He tried to remember a time when he might have felt differently. And as though his footsteps were being guided, he came upon an item that would trigger a memory.

Standing in front of an item covered in heavy muslin canvas G-tang removed the cover. Standing before him was a dust-covered full-length mirror. The dust was so thick G-Tang wiped an area of the mirror clean with his hand. When he did, webs of dust clung to his fingers.

Staring back at him was a spitting image of a younger version of his father. He smiled at G-Tang. It was a smile filled with joy. A smile carved and crafted, well before the street games of life set in. He smiled a smile G-Tang remembered from when he was a young boy.

In that instant it was a smile meant only for him. G-Tang instinctively reached out to touch the smile on the handsome face as his heart yearned for something that had been lost to him for a long time.

As soon as his fingers made contact with the glass G-Tang found himself as a young boy of five, being twirled in his father's arms. His mother gazed at them adoringly.

The room was gaily decorated and warm with the presence of Christmas. Lights were twinkling on the tree; they lit up the windows in a sparkling glow. G-Tang, his dad, and his mom were dancing to the sound of Michael Jackson singing. "I Saw Mommy Kissing Santa Claus."

They danced and danced around and around.

Chance reached over to kiss a much younger and slimmer Beatrice. Pure love for him shone brightly from her eyes. Then she reached over and chucked her son under the chin, smiling warmly into his eyes.

His dad then planted a kiss on G-Tang's forehead. G-Tang hugged his father's neck and never wanted to let go. He could feel the warm pulse beating in his neck. G-Tang kissed the vibrating spot as his dad tickled him, sending him into a gale of giggles.

Alas, one day the music stopped. The twinkling lights no longer twinkled. The bells on the tree no longer tinkled. The beautiful branches on the Christmas tree lost their ornaments, dried up and died. All that would be left of their time together was *the* memory.

The morning he woke up to discover his father was gone was one that would live within him for a very long time. The memory of the last Christmas they'd spent was all he had. That was the day that he began to hate Christmas. Christmas for him was a dim and painful memory.

In fact Christmas for him was no more. Where there should have been love, there was hate. Where there should have been joy, there was sorrow.

The place left in his heart for those emotions, was now only hollow.

And that was just the way it was. For G-Tang, Christmas had died long ago.

Thou Shalt Not Take the Name of the Lord, Thy God in Vain

Standing in the ancient cemetery once again, the Spirit of Discernment and the Spirit of Innocence heard a sorrowful moaning as though the notes were floating from the sound of a flute, illustrating the depths of its pain.

This they heard instead of the familiar *ka-chunk* they had come to expect.

Following the sound of the flute they were led into the lowest depths of a black pit filled with nothing more than human despair. They saw people roaming a city block.

The most startling thing about the people was that they had no respect for God, none whatsoever. Their disrespect was written in spirit. Discernment and Sam could see it clearly, while the people were oblivious to their very own actions.

This commandment unlike the ones that had come before it, and had thundered out their meanings, simply inscribed itself into one of the city's brick walls, splashed like graffiti.

The Spirit of Discernment and the Spirit of Innocence exchanged looks at the appearance of the inscription.

"That wasn't even as loud as a whisper," the Spirit of Innocence remarked. Before he could say anything further a woman's voice called out, "God damn it!"

Discernment flinched in his spirit at the blatant disrespect. He hurt in a deep place because he knew how carelessly and nonchalantly people used that phrase, unknowingly offending God.

It was the same thing when men or women called out the name Jesus Christ, with the same intent, as a curse rather than as a form of praise.

"Oh, don't you know? Can't you feel it?" Discernment asked softly, saddened at the way they used the precious name of the Lord to swear.

Suddenly as though they were watching a sneak preview of a high-profile movie to come, Discernment and Sam were allowed to look past the flesh, observing only the spirit of the people.

The spirit is the life force directly connecting man with God, and has been so ever since the first man was created, when God blew the *breath of life* into him.

The spirit's animation when separated from flesh was quite a sight and essence to behold. The two angels, though heavy of heart at what they were seeing, marveled at the creation of a life force that was similar to a separate entity, much the same as when people die and the spirit separates from the flesh. Though the body was dead, the spirit still has life, and at that moment they viewed the spoilage of the human spirit.

All of these people had taken the Lord's name in vain, and not one believed in his or her own creator. All they saw was the physical, the flesh. For them dead was *dead.* In essence by taking the name of the Lord in vain, and not being receptive in their spirits to the very creator of their life force, they had sealed their own fates.

Sam was the first to spot the mist of the Spirit moving once again, amongst them like a wave washed ashore. They went on about their everyday lives, oblivious to the disrespect and dishonor they had created and shown their maker.

But then again most of them hadn't respected their own flesh either. There would be the coming of the *Second Death* as written and spoken of in the Book of Revelations.

"Thou Shalt Not Take the Name of the Lord, Thy God, in Vain!" This time the words boomed angrily from the heavens, and immediately that sorrowful note they had heard earlier came soaring from the flute once again, penetrating their midst, attaching itself to the spirit so that at least someone would feel the pain of the Lord Jesus Christ, of his forgotten love, of his father God, and last but not at all least, of the Holiness of the Spirit.

The Spirit mist traveled like a giant.

Sam sucked in a breath. He wanted to look at Discernment to seek comfort, but found that he couldn't.

Suddenly the scene changed.

The Spirit of Innocence saw Jamie in the store on the corner of Albany Avenue and Edgewood Street. She was buying candy.

A young woman who was really just a skeleton of who she once was was also in the store. She was addicted to crack cocaine and it had a serious grip on her, it was the ruling force in her life.

All of this was obvious in the space of a nanosecond.

She dropped a quarter on the floor and swore, "God damn it." She bent to retrieve the quarter, with great difficulty, moving like she was eighty instead of twenty-eight.

Jamie turned to her and said, "You shouldn't take the Lord's name in vain. It isn't nice."

As high as she was the woman fixed her eyes steadily on Jamie who was now facing her waiting patiently for an apology. The woman was so angry she could taste the salt of venom in her response before the words actually left her mouth.

But in fact the words never left her mouth as Jamie returned her stare.

The Spirit mist enclosed and surrounded the store as Jamie stared unwaveringly at the woman, holding both her ground and her position. Not one soul could have entered that store at that time.

The woman looked into the depths of Jamie's eyes. Instead of scorn she witnessed compassion, and the depths of a love she'd never seen or beheld before.

She hesitated, swallowing hard and finally in a childlike whisper she said, "I'm sorry."

The owner of the store took a step back in astonishment. Before he could digest what he'd witnessed, Jamie threw her arms around the woman and said, "Jesus loves you. I know he does."

Right then and there at the sound of the Messiah's name, one of the most hardened drug addicts in the city of Hartford bowed her head in shame, vowing in her heart never to take the Lord's name in vain again.

Then she broke down weeping.

The same sorrowful weeping that Discernment and Sam had heard from the flute, now flowed from this woman's lips.

The Spirit mist turned to a gentle breeze.

Sam, the Spirit of Innocence, was learning. He remembered the Lord's words, "If there be one," spoken long ago in the time of Lot and the Pillar of Salt.

"If there be one," the Spirit mist uttered as it took its leave.

Jamie sat in the middle of the floor, her candy forgotten, holding the weeping woman in her arms, rocking her back and forth as though she were the child. And for the moment she was. In the instant she had opened her heart to the spirit of Christ, her heart had become mired in the innocence of a child and she had apologized for her actions.

Jamie continued to rock the weeping woman, holding her close. The comfort the woman felt in that one little child's arms was something she'd never be able to describe in her lifetime.

The woman's name was Carmen.

Before Christmas would end, which is a glorious time for miracles, Carmen would stand before the doors of the church before they opened waiting to be let in, her spirit as white as a dove, her eyes transfixed on the cross of Jesus Christ. Her crack addition would be a thing of the past.

Such is the reward for following God's laws.

Thou Shalt Not Take the Name of the Lord, Thy God, in Vain.

Sam finally turned to look at Discernment and found the elder angel, dabbing at his wet eyes.

He turned once again to find they were back on the city street. He stood watching the words disappear from the wall.

Thou Shalt Not Take the Name of the Lord, Thy God, in Vain.

Sam nodded his understanding.

The Art of Giving

The shelter for battered women and their children was full. The location was kept secret for the safety of the women and their children.

So it was a strict rule that anyone affiliated with the shelter vowed to keep its location a secret.

Every year Jamie's Grandma Lizzie volunteered her services and took Jamie along with her. They did their best to spread cheer and goodwill among the women and children.

Each year they brought platters of food. They also brought new warm clothing such as hats, gloves, earmuffs, scarves, and snowsuits for the kids as well as clothing for the women with the money George would give them to share with others. And share they did.

And, of course, Lizzie was always on kitchen duty.

Miz Taylor could also be counted on as well

to bring the sweet potato pies. The shelter's location was one secret she could keep.

Miz Taylor spotted Lizzie and Jamie Lynne as
soon as she walked in. She made it her business
to have a word with Lizzie. She wished she had
married a man like George, instead of the bum
who had beat her senseless, landing her in the
hospital.

Her physical wounds had healed, but the
wounds in her heart never would.

"Well, Lizzie," Miz Taylor greeted her. "Another season it is. And here we are again."

Lizzie gathered Miz Taylor's stiff body in her
arms, enveloping her in her warm bulk. She knew
all about her past, as well as Miz Taylor's envy
and crush on her husband, but she didn't mind.

She was safe and secure in her marriage. As
well she wished Miz Taylor would find love and
happiness in her life. It might be possible if
she'd chastise that caustic tongue of hers, sometimes.

Hugging her warmly Lizzie said, "'Tis the season it is, Ellie. And a time for miracles it is too.
I've got a feeling this year we're going to see
quite a few miracles, but all we need is one."

Miz Taylor withstood the hug then pulled
back to look at Lizzie. "Well, it's a miracle that I
finished all those pies, that's for sure!"

She made a small snorting sound. "You know
my arthritis started to flare up, but I kept right
on, and just said, 'Devil you're a liar.' "

"So, how's George during this wonderful
holiday?"

Lizzie smiled. She was gracious in her accep-
tance of Ellie's crush on her husband. "He's

fine, Ellie. Thanks for asking. You'll catch a glimpse of him I'm sure at the Christmas services."

Miz Taylor had the grace to blush. "Well, I hope so. It'll be nice to see him," she finished respectfully.

Just then Jamie bounded up tugging on Lizzie's skirt. "Grandma Lizzie, come meet my new friends," Jamie said excitedly. "Hi, Miz Taylor."

Miz Taylor was still in a huff with Jamie over the mistletoe episode in Mr. Mitchell's store, so she was somewhat reserved with Jamie.

She didn't know what Lizzie and George were teaching that child, but they needed to bring her down to earth. If Jamie had been her grandchild she wouldn't have allowed her to run around spouting things in public like waiting for Jesus.

"Hello, Jamie Lynne," she said. Then as an afterthought, "You know if I were you I wouldn't go around telling the other kids that story about waiting on Jesus to bring you a miracle. Not everybody cottons to that kind of stuff."

From the lifting of her shoulders, it was obvious Miz Taylor felt as though she had passed on good advice.

Lizzie's eyes widened, and twinkled in defense of her granddaughter. "Why believing is half the miracle. You know that, Ellie."

"Miz Taylor, it looks like somebody likes your pies." Jamie pointed in the direction of a young boy who had just stuck his finger in one of Miz Taylor's perfectly crafted pies, and was now sucking his finger with his eyes closed as the smooth blend of cinnamon, nutmeg, butter, and vanilla cruised down his throat. He had a look of pure pleasure written across his face.

Miz Taylor hurried toward him in a huff. "Young man, do not stick your finger in that pie."

Jamie laughed.

So did Lizzie; she couldn't help herself. It was a sight to see the child looking so blissfully happy at his taste of sweetness, and Ellie with a scowl on her face racing to chastise him.

She absolutely hated anyone to touch her pies, and everyone knew it. She didn't allow anyone to slice them either.

Still Lizzie admonished Jamie. "That wasn't quite nice, Jamie!"

Jamie smiled once again. "I know, Grandma Lizzie. I'm sorry. But Miz Taylor doesn't believe in anything. She's like a wet rag being thrown over a warm, crackling fire."

At this statement Lizzie threw her head back in laughter at the sheer truth of that statement. "Okay. You're right. But remember you must always be polite."

"I will, Grandma Lizzie. I promise I will." Jamie let out a squeal as she spotted her most favorite adult, Mr. Mitchell, wandering through the door, his arms laden with candy canes, candy apples, bags of sugar, eggs, and all kinds of goodies for the women and children in the shelter.

Lizzie smiled at him and waved, as Jamie ran over. Lizzie made her way back to the kitchen where she was baking cinnamon cookies along with her famous snowball cookies, which she would soon need to roll in confectioners' sugar while they were still warm.

"Mr. Mitchell, you're here." Jamie practically pounced on him. He put his bags on the nearest counter, lifting her in his arms, planting a kiss on her cheek.

"I am and so are you."

"Of course I am, Mr. Mitchell. I come here every year. You know that."

"I sho' do. That's why I'm here." He smiled.

"No it's not. You're here to give goodies to everybody."

"You wanna help?"

"Yep," she smiled her answer, sticking her hand in one of the bags, grabbing a handful of candy canes, and running off to pass them out. Passing out Mr. Mitchell's goodies and seeing the looks on the other kids' faces was part of her favorite reason for coming to the shelter.

Mr. Mitchell knew it. That's why he always let her distribute to the kids. Jamie loved the art of giving. She walked around the shelter sharing her own brand of warmth, adding a bit of light, cheer, and laughter to others who were less fortunate than she.

She'd also spent her saved allowances to pass out one very special gift this Christmas. It was wrapped in a soft red cloth that she'd gotten from a visit to the fabric shop with her grandma Lizzie. She'd hand cut the cloth herself to fit the size of her gifts. Nestled in the center of the cloths were little wooden crosses she'd bought. Beneath the cross sewn in ragged stitching, with her own hand were the words, "Jesus loves you!"

Jamie handed them out to the women and children with a smile.

Sam smiled in Discernment's direction as he saw a little boy open the red cloth Jamie had given him, read the words, then look up at Jamie saying, "He does? Who's Jesus?"

Jamie put her arm around the boy. He was about six and just learning to read. She sat next to him to explain.

Sam said to Discernment, "I guess I shouldn't have been too worried about her ancestral genes and all, huh?"

"I guess not," Discernment said with his arms folded as he listened to Jamie say, "Jesus Christ is the light of the world."

22

Drip. Drip. Drip.

Cynthia sat listening to her prison counselor's voice. She had quite a struggle focusing. She kept hearing the constant drip of the water.

Drip. Drip. Drip.

Try as she might, she couldn't tune out the sound of that dripping. She hugged herself as Sylvia, her counselor, searched her unfocused eyes, wondering if she'd heard a word she'd said.

Sylvia shook her head in annoyance. "Cynthia, are you listening to me? Trips to the hole are not the way to get out of prison to see your daughter."

"I know that," Cynthia muttered.

The hole had been one of the nastiest, filthiest, darkest places she had ever occupied in her life. She had no desire to visit again. Her arms still carried the red welts from where she had pinched herself.

Yet even though the constant dripping of that

water had almost driven her insane, she had found a sort of soothing comfort in the consistency of it.

Nothing with the exception of her baby girl, Jamie Lynne, had ever been a constant in her life. Her dad had always tried to provide that for her, but she'd been rebellious toward all of his efforts.

She bit her tongue just as she was tempted to tell Sylvia about the constant rhythm of the water dripping in the hole. And how she had been able to piece together reflections of herself because of it.

She stopped herself just in time from blurting out the words that wouldn't have been believed. Sylvia would have though she was sliding over the edge.

It was a good thing she hadn't blurted it out because an investigation of her place of solitary confinement would have revealed nothing except silence. There wasn't a drop of water there or anywhere near where she had been imprisoned.

As deep as that dungeon was, there had never been a drop of water in it.

Yet Cynthia had heard it, and when she didn't want to claw at the walls because of the constant drip, drip, drip, she'd seen her own flaws and vowed to God, if he was listening, to do better.

She didn't know if he was listening, but she did know for sure he was there. She'd known it at some level ever since her daughter had been placed in her arms.

"That trip to the hole is going to set you back

in time. There's no way you'll be home in time for Christmas that I can see. Barring a miracle, there just isn't much I can do. Your behavior has tied my hands."

Cynthia's lower lip trembled. She was on the verge of tears, but prison was a place where tears could get you killed.

"I've got to be there this Christmas for my baby. You know that fight wasn't my fault. It isn't fair," Cynthia challenged.

"Life seldom is," Sylvia sighed. "I'm sorry."

Cynthia pulled her knees up to her chin. Once again she heard the drip, drip, drip of that water and she wasn't even in the hole now. It just kept dripping, and dripping, and dripping. Try as she might, she could not shut out that sound.

She stared out the window at the miles of nothingness, just fields of grass that surrounded the prison. She could see a little bit of a cloudless blue sky.

Somehow she knew her answer lay in that water she kept hearing, dripping. It was trying to tell her something.

Before she could stop them the words popped out of her mouth. "Sometimes you can't pay attention to these laws. You gotta go directly to the Lord."

Cynthia rose from her seat, a secret smile touching her lips, as she realized what she had to do.

Sam and Discernment exchanged a brief smile from their position on the windowsill.

That night found Cynthia Brooks on her knees praying, "Our Father who art in heaven," she began.

Sharese F. Brooks

Sharese was all glitter on the outside, but on the inside she was distraught and out of contact. She had been flying on automatic pilot for months and the only thing that had saved her from a complete crash was her penchant for organization and her gift of a photographic memory. Once an object passed before Sharese's eye, it locked in her mind, and she could recall it at will.

Thank the Lord for his miracles.

She was a high-flying chief financial officer in a premier, well-respected insurance company. Yet, she felt like she was one misstep away from emotional disaster. It was only by a miracle and sheer grace that thus far no one had noticed, or so she thought.

She had a love/hate relationship with her own life. On the one hand she loved what she did. She'd always had an affinity for numbers.

She loved the respect she garnered in her position, as well as the awe she garnered being a Black female in her position. Although that phrase someone had coined about it being lonely at the top was nothing but truth.

Yet, there was no way anyone could know the burden that Sharese F. Brooks carried. The *F* she'd never told anyone about, stood for Frances, which she secretly loathed. Ugh.

There was no way people could know how heavy a burden it was being young, gifted, Black, female, financially capable, and a member of a family who only saw your outside achievements, but never once thought you might have an emotional need of your own.

Nope.

She was good ole Sharese, a credit to her race, a credit in the public eye to the family name, dependable for both personal and financial needs as they arose in the family.

And Beatrice never let her forget about all the sacrifices that had been made, and how she would be forever indebted to her brother, George, for ensuring a Spelman College education for Sharese, without any financial difficulties attached.

To add to her list of credits, Sharese was known to be a good listener, a great shoulder that other people could cry on, and she would take a secret to her deathbed, out of loyalty. Nothing short of torture would get any secret out of her.

And last, but not least, she was an overachiever. An overachiever who was only a stone's throw away from a major breakdown.

Smokey Robinson's "The Tears of a Clown" was on repeat on her CD player. Though it was an old school jam, and a song not of her own generation, it accurately described her to a T.

She was always well put together and smiling on the outside, but on the inside her heart was breaking. She'd cried herself to sleep many a night.

The one bright spot in her life was her young cousin, Jamie. Thinking about her brought a smile to her lips. Jamie was special. Sharese didn't know how Jamie was special; she just knew she was.

Sharese was drawn to Jamie on a level she didn't quite understand.

In her own special way, Jamie gave Sharese an emotional balance in her life. Sharese often wished Jamie was her daughter.

Sharese had spent an inordinate amount of time selecting special gifts for Jamie for Christmas, but she was the one who *really* needed a gift.

If she had one wish for Christmas it would be for peace. Yes, she needed a way to accept herself for who and what she was. She needed to learn not to be afraid of who she was, and instinctively she knew that finding that particular road could lead her to peace.

Jamie tossed and turned in her sleep where she saw her cousin Sharese standing before a Christmas tree laden with gifts, and not finding one with her name on it.

Jamie saw the track of a tear slip from one of Sharese's eyes. Her own heart grew heavy. "Sharese," she called out in her sleep.

Sam bowed his head at the sadness with which Jamie had called Sharese's name.

24

Beatrice Brooks

Beatrice Brooks was pushing hard at sixty's door, and at fifty-nine, she hadn't learned or accepted most of life's basic lessons.

Beatrice had essentially lived her life hard, fast, and fun loving, without thought for the future or the consequences of her actions.

She could drink the average man under the table, and she was still known to close a bar or two in Hartford, though not to the degree she had when she was younger.

"Last night three drive-by shootings left three African-American males, their ages ranging from fifteen to seventeen, dead in the vicinity of Vine Street," the reporter's voice droned from the television.

Beatrice clicked the mute button, leaving only silent images. She was sick and damned tired of the nonsense in Hartford. How the hell couldn't a city that had the kind of insurance industry money that Hartford had not be able to stop these kids from killing each other?

She'd bet her bottom dollar if they went over to West Hartford, land of the affluent, with that nonsense they'd find a way to stop it, in a heart-beat.

That's why she had ceased donating to the police union. What the hell were they doing downtown? They'd better restructure all that front street politicking, so they could do some-thing about this madness. All that damned postur-ing wasn't getting anything done.

On that thought she strode over to the minibar, helping herself to a straight shot of J&B.

The only one of her children that she wor-ried about getting caught up in that madness was David. She had two others who were slipping in and out of the cracks, but this information was unbeknownst to her.

Beatrice knew for a fact David had a love af-fair with both the darkest parts of the hood and drugs. She had infiltrated his life on the streets and paid informants to discover just how in-volved he was.

It was deep.

She had discovered to her heartbreak that he was just like his daddy in that respect.

You could take David's dad out of the ghetto, but you couldn't take the ghetto out of him. Pe-riod.

It was a crying shame, fine as he was. All that fineness was wasting away in the federal peni-tentiary. *There should be a law against that.* She never even went to see him. What was the point? The man was doing *life*. She'd never hold him, or lay next to him again.

On the day he was incarcerated something inside of her died. And she considered him as good as dead too. They got him on drug trafficking charges. He was a career criminal. A three-time loser, and that was it.

She shivered and then poured herself two straight shots. She hit the intercom button, "David!"

There was no answer.

"David!" she screamed again, only louder and more boisterous.

G-Tang appeared in his pajamas.

"What the hell you sneaking up on me for? Why didn't you just answer?"

"I'm answering now, Ma. What do you want?"

Really, she hadn't wanted anything except to see his face. He was approaching eighteen, and she hoped that would take him out of the danger zone in Hartford.

These days if a kid lived to eighteen, he was almost past the death and execution stage that had besieged the city.

"Can you get me some bottled water?" Beatrice asked.

G-Tang reached behind the bar and sat a bottle of Evian in front of her.

He was no fool. He knew she didn't want anything. And he hoped like hell after seeing the shot glass in her hand that she wasn't about to go on one of her crying jags.

He was the last child at home, and many a

night he had put his mother to bed after she had drunk herself into a stupor.

Beatrice looked at him content and happy to just see his face, the face of his father. "Thanks," she said woodenly.

G-Tang turned to leave. "Tang," she said before he could go.

G-Tang couldn't believe his ears. He was shocked. She'd never, ever, called him anything except David, which he secretly despised, as well as considered a lack of respect since he liked to be called by the name that repped him best.

"Yeah?" he said disguising his shock.

"You know I love you. Right?"

He gave her a small smile. Inside he knew she was crazy about him, and he sometimes took advantage of that. But deep down inside, he loved her too, much more than she probably knew.

The tough exterior that she showed the world wasn't always shown to him, particularly when it was just the two of them. He saw a vulnerability and softness in her that most people didn't realize existed.

With the shock of that thought, he realized he saw that side of her, because she trusted in him.

"Yeah, Ma. I know that."

She downed another straight shot before focusing on him.

"Good," she finally said. She walked over to hug him briefly. The tear in her eye didn't fall. She said a private prayer, really it was more like a private begging, that God would please not let the fate of his father fall on her son.

She figured since God had a son of his own, he might pay attention to this particular prayer. She certainly hoped it would get his attention. After all it *was* Christmas.

"Get out of here," she brushed him off, so she could be alone again.

She harbored a desire to be alone with her memories of David's father, and her and little David, happy at a Christmas long, long ago.

She looked over at the sparkling tree, the space beneath filled with every present imaginable. They looked so meaningless to her as she was flooded with memories of Christmas past.

She clicked a switch turning on the musical lights that played Christmas songs.

She was met with the melody to "The First Noel." The lyrics poured forth in her mind:

The First Noel, the Angels did say, was to certain poor shepherds in fields as they lay. In fields where they lay keeping their sheep, on a cold winter's night that was so deep. Noel, Noel, Noel, Noel. Born is the King of Israel!

She wished she could meet or at least feel the King of Israel, if in fact he really existed. She ruminated, thinking of a possible savior for herself.

She was overcome with a strange feeling as though there were something she should be remembering, but couldn't quite recall. It had something to do with being at George's for the pre-Christmas breakfast. A dream or something that she'd had.

She stood there watching the flashing, twinkling colors on the tree and listening to the melody.

If she'd had one Christmas wish, it would have been that she would stop drinking, so she could feel again.

She was growing tired of being numb.

Feeling her pain, the Spirit of Innocence who was making his rounds throughout the family now, accelerating his presence in Jamie's life, sprinkled gold sawdust over Beatrice's head. He then promptly tripped over a box under the Christmas tree, as he was walking to the staircase that led upstairs.

This time Discernment only smiled.

Before they left they had one more visit to make. They needed to ensure David would return to the attic and open the dust-covered box, when the time came.

Dwayne Brooks

Dwayne was one gorgeous hunk of a man on the outside.

God doesn't make mistakes, and it was too bad Dwayne thought he had when it came to his manhood, because it had hindered him from being the man he could truly be, and it had thrown a blanket of darkness over his life.

He was essentially living the life of a person with a split personality. He was walking the line between two sexualities. In the process his true self was being stilted, and the loathing he was experiencing because of his double life was crippling.

Dwayne looked in the mirror, distraught with the picture of perfect handsomeness that stared back at him. He obliterated the image with a black eyeliner pencil he was holding.

He could no longer stand the face, nor the image, that looked back at him. Worst of all, he no longer knew which face belonged to him, the masculine or the feminine.

Exhausted from his assault on the mirror, he sat down on top of the toilet seat, putting his head in his hands. He felt the migraine fast approaching and knew he'd spend the rest of the day in blackness, no light, eyes shut, with a cool cloth to his head, lying still, trying not to move a muscle.

The slightest movement would inflict pain.

Hours later as predicted, Dwayne lay prone, perfectly still. Over time he'd learned to be as still as the Silver Tin Man in New York City, the one who worked the Times Square circuit. He only moved if you dropped money in his tin can, box, or bucket, whichever means of capturing cash he had chosen to use for the day.

When he went to New York Dwayne used to marvel at this dude. He'd found it hard to believe this cat really didn't move, so he'd spent some time watching him.

He'd come away knowing the cat was authentic.

He did not move, not a muscle, unless you laid some cash on him. And his movements were in direct contrast with how much cash you laid on him. If you dropped only coins, you got a twitch here or there. If you laid down some bills, then you were treated to a wonderful world of well-choreographed movement.

When the performance ended the Silver Tin Man resumed his static position. And, that is the way he stayed, until the next influx of cash came his way.

At the time Dwayne was studying the Silver Tin Man he hadn't known he'd need this particular skill to survive the afflicting pain of migraines.

He'd in fact been in the city on the down low, blending into the hybrid of the culture where nobody knew him.

It was all good, until he questioned his sexuality, hence the migraines had come upon him, attacking him with a vengeance.

He had discovered early on that he had something people coveted, worshipped even, if it were presented to them in the right light, and that was flesh, pound for pound.

Good looking, sinewy, sexy, perfectly shaped and molded, flesh. What he hadn't known originally, but had stumbled on almost by accident, was that his face and body appealed to both sexes.

There were men who would pay, and pay, and pay, as well as support his extravagant lifestyle for the mere privilege of looking, touching, and being in his sphere.

He learned rather quickly where the *true* money brokers were, as well as where they feasted, and it became his new, very lucrative career.

Dwayne had accumulated homes, vehicles, jewelry, cash, a 401k plan, stock, and he'd even been given old, blue chip stocks in one of America's premier 500 companies by a man whose face frequently graced the pages of the business media.

Dwayne wasn't fond of recalling the exact price by which he'd come by the blue chip stocks.

It was a memory better off buried. The payment had been extremely high. The kind of payment that seared one's soul.

Dwayne was somewhat paranoid. He'd had a strong trait of self-preservation, so his goal had always been to have everything meticulously paid for, and in his name, just in case trouble ever came.

The end of a relationship would never cost him a quiver of financial hardship, nor any kind of disaster, he had vowed. And he managed to keep his word.

These guys played by his rules or he didn't play. No game, no shame. It was working nicely until he made the mistake of hooking up in the city with one of the elite members from his own community and stomping grounds. Everyone knew you didn't play in your own backyard, everyone, except Dwayne that is.

So, in the midst of this choice, which only held drama and trauma, he'd been cleaning the depths of his bedroom closet one day, and trust this as an accurate description, that's how deep his closets were, that they possessed depths, when he plucked a book from the blackest corner, and sat mesmerized staring at a pair of old, wizened, Black hands, folded over one another, atop the Holy Bible.

He'd honestly never seen a pair of black hands covering the Bible, and for the life of him he couldn't place where the Bible had come from. He didn't even own a Bible, and hadn't seen one since he was a child, made to go to church on Sunday, primarily due to his grandmother's nagging. Hattie Brooks always got her own way.

He wondered if perhaps it had come from Beatrice's house, which was the private term in which he thought of his alcoholic mother. He always thought of her by her first name for some reason. He never called her by her first name to her face, but that was how he thought of her.

In any case he couldn't be sure the Bible had come from Beatrice's house, but he didn't have a better answer.

He was sure of only one thing.

From the instant he had touched it, and opened its gilded pages to read the text written in red, he'd been in emotional agony, and hence the migraines he now lived with.

For the first time in his privileged life, he had examined himself and his lust for all things material, and he didn't like what he had seen. The man in the mirror.

Such was his quandary that with the exception of the one relationship that was left to be extinguished, he had severed all ties to the down low community or *DL*, the acronym by which it was now becoming known.

The behavior, lifestyle, and emotional syndromes attached to being on the down low, had spread like a forest fire throughout the country.

It also had whole families running scared, in fear of their very lives, as they tried to dodge AIDS.

He spent an inordinate amount of time in prayer, and in the continued study of the red text, and as such he had become the victim of vicious migraines.

His conflicting flesh was lashing back at him.

Yet, despite the pain and despite the agony of

his torn emotions, he could not deny the profound peace, or the feeling of being connected at a higher level whenever he touched that book.

Bit by bit he had been cleansing his life.

Now the melody to "The First Noel" penetrated his psyche, as the migraine finally subsided. He smiled in memory of always hearing the melody playing on the Christmas tree, at his family's home every year.

Relieved at being able to turn his head without hot searing pain, he peered through the darkness at the silent tree, realizing for the first time that every single year he had been duplicating the Christmases of his childhood in his own home.

Still not ready to move, in his mind's eye he saw the twinkling Christmas tree of his past, and heard the melodic song, as it had played then, "The First Noel!"

If he had had one wish for Christmas it would have been that he could lay his burden down, so he could be whole, and face the Lord without shame.

The Lord didn't make mistakes, he'd finally learned. It was he who had made the mistake.

Yet he knew the Lord was great and merciful, he could feel the power of that in his life urging him onward, even as he struggled to do what was right.

He knew in his heart he was not forsaken.

Sam looked at the cousin that Jamie loved so much. Being the Spirit of Innocence, he was al-

ways able to spot that particular trait of innocence, as it manifested in someone else.

Deep in Dwayne's heart he still had it. *Innocence.*

He hadn't enjoyed and pursued his lifestyle
without guilt or conscience. Instead he had been
mightily conflicted because of it. He had struggled to understand, stared the most flawed part
of himself in the face, and then sought another
way.

The Spirit of Innocence touched Dwayne
lightly on his chest. The Spirit of Discernment
nodded.

The two angels headed toward the door,
though not before Sam tripped over one of
Dwayne's slippers in the dark. When he did the
light that was shed on the entire area was something to behold.

26

The Purpose

Jamie sat watching Hattie sift through hat-boxes. Her great-grandmother was one of the grand dames of hat wearing. An old tried-and-true hat diva.

She seemed to own every style or type of hat imaginable, or created.

Jamie peered into a cedar closet that her grandfather had had built in Hattie's house to hold nothing but her hats. The closet was the size of a small bedroom and it was deep.

On its shelves sat hats, primly, proudly, and sometimes extravagantly in their boxes, awaiting an opportunity to portray the moment by shining in splendor atop Hattie's head.

There were feathered hats and ostrich hats, there was even a hat made from kangaroo hide. Hattie had them in velvet, silk, wool, cashmere, in every, shape size, and color.

eBay didn't have anything on Hattie when it

came to discovering some of the world's greatest hats.

"Lord have mercy," Hattie said looking at the array of hats that were overwhelming even to her at times, especially today.

"How am I ever going to choose?"

"I don't know, Grandma," Jamie smiled. "But you'd better choose soon or you're going to be late for the Woman's Committee meeting at church."

"Hush now, child. You have no idea what you're talking about," Hattie huffed, frazzled that she couldn't decide on the right hat.

Jamie said nothing more. She just glanced over at the clock and smiled.

Hattie sighed. It was imperative that she chose the right hat, particularly today. She was chair of the committee, and she needed a hat that reflected dominance, and extracted a let's-get-down-to-business attitude but yet gave off grace and style.

She didn't want to come across as aggressive, just ambitious, in flight to her goal.

Her topic today was the death of the young Black males in the city. The ones that had no one to speak for them during that despicable newscast she'd seen, where all the reporter did was show an aerial shot of the area where the murders took place, but didn't have one Black voice to cry out publicly against such an insult and outrage.

It was absolutely intolerable that these children were killing each other. And the church could not stand idly by watching the loss of an entire generation, or at least Hattie couldn't.

So, she had marshaled and ushered her woman's group into an emergency meeting to address the issue.

She had had to practically move heaven and earth, despite the direness of the circumstances, to hold this meeting because people wanted to go Christmas shopping. Imagine!

These people called themselves saints, yet they had trouble getting their priorities straight. Jesus hadn't died up there on that cross for nothing. She hadn't stood for that nonsense, hence the Women's Committee meeting today.

Finally she spied the hat she wanted. She lifted it carefully from its box and stuck it regally on top of her head.

She stood before the full-length mirror knowing it was a perfect fit for the occasion before her. The hat had black hand-sewn ostrich feathers, it was small, tightly fitted, and it had a dropdown veil that covered her eyes, and fell just below the tip of the nose.

Most people didn't wear veiled hats anymore, but she was not most people.

The structure of the hat gave it just the right amount of severity, yet suited her entire purpose. It was also an asset, as well as a striking match, for her black suit with the silver buttons, cuffs, and accessories.

Jamie looked startled as she took in the final effect the hat had on her great-grandmother. "Grandma, you look like you're going to a funeral, but like you're there for business."

"That's right, baby. Somebody's got to be about the business of mourning those children in the spirit, and bringing the ignorance of our ways to the forefront of our minds. There definitely needs to be a funeral for ignorance."

Hattie took Jamie's hand, pulling her up off the floor, and firmly shut the cedar closet door.

"Jamie go call the car for grandma."

"Yes, Grandma," Jamie said. And in her heart she vowed one day, she'd be a sojourner for truth, just like her grandma was.

Sojourner was the last word she'd learned on her vocabulary test, just before school adjourned for Christmas vacation.

Jamie decided she liked the taste of the word on her tongue. Maybe she'd make a poem out of it. Sojourner. Yes, she'd be a sojourner for truth when she grew up.

Jamie smiled in her great-grandmother's direction as she called the car.

27

If There Be One

When Hattie reached the church, she went directly to the lounge area, where she knew she would find the women in her group. With the exception of one they had all managed to shuffle their shopping and baking schedules to be in attendance.

Hattie shuddered in her soul as she realized the missing committee member had lost one of her very own grandsons three years ago to street violence and she hadn't even bothered to show up for the meeting.

"Mercy me," Hattie said aloud.

"What?" one of the women asked.

"Nothing," Hattie replied as she stood looking them over.

Surveying the lounge, she said, "We're going to have this meeting in the pastor's study." Her tone brooked no argument. The women looked a bit startled, since they had situated themselves and were comfortable.

And that was precisely the point. She didn't want these ladies comfortable, she wanted them uncomfortable, and on point. This was not a comfortable situation.

Hattie had always been a natural-born leader. And she possessed presence. When she spoke most people listened. At her instruction the six of them filed off to sit around the conference table, with the hard-back chairs in the pastor's study.

Before leaving the lounge, Hattie said a prayer for her missing committee member that the Lord would put it on her heart to attend the meeting. Running had never solved anything. Sometimes you had to look evil in the face, and be ready to fight for what was right.

As she stood before the conference table officially bringing the meeting to order, one of the women, after taking in her apparel, remarked, "You look as if you're going to a funeral, Hattie."

Hattie fixed her eyes on the woman, tilting her head imperially. "I think ten Black boys shot and killed in one night is a time for mourning. Don't you?"

The woman bowed her head and nodded.

Sister Jackson spoke up, "Well, what do you want us to do?"

"What do you think we should do?" Hattie shot back, as she lowered herself into the hard chair, trying not to visibly flinch from the discomfort of it.

She placed her hands over her African-American Heritage King James Bible for the needed strength and support. Whenever she came into contact with the word of Christ it strengthened her.

This particular Bible was special to her. It had been ever since she had discovered it on a trip to Harlem and she learned the history behind the life of the Black man who made its publication possible.

Her beloved version was the African-American Heritage King James Bible, edited by James Peebles, and published by the James C. Winston Publishing Company. She'd never used another Bible since. Its appendix contained the Old Negro Spirituals, which was something special for her.

Sister Jackson's voice penetrated her thoughts. "Ain't much we can do," she answered in her most annoying voice. "These kids don't listen to us."

Hattie didn't care to hear the excuses. "Then we'd better get them to listen. Cuz we're losing them as though we're in some kind of war."

Precisely in that instant the last committee member stumbled through the door.

Tears ran down her face. Her pantyhose were ripped from falling and black streaks of mascara ran from her eyes, in rivulets down her cheeks, coupling with red spots of streaming rouge.

Her bottom lip trembled as she looked at the group of assembled women, and then finally at Hattie, as she struggled valiantly to get the words out. "I . . . I . . . wasn't gon' come today. Because I'm just so sick and tired of it all."

She hesitated, swallowed, and then continued as her eyes found the cross of Jesus Christ, hanging all alone on the wall.

Her fingers, without any will of her own, reached out toward the cross. She took a tentative step in the direction of the wall that was holding the nailed cross.

When she reached the cross she stretched her fingers toward it. When she touched it, she left a spot of blood, from her bleeding hand.

Speechless, she stood with pain racking her body and tears streaming down her face. Finally, she forced out more words. "I run all the way to the church." Her southern accent was strongly pronounced, as it was whenever she was really upset.

Touching the blood-stained cross again, she whispered, "They done took another one of my grandsons. Somebody shot and killed him. They done left him in Keney Park."

Her voice dropped. They all sat forward in their seats straining to hear her.

"His body is riddled with bullets. They done destroyed him. Ain't gon' be able to open the casket. Just yesterday he brought the apples from Stop-N-Shop for me to bake my pies for Christmas. Blood done signed my family's name.

"My . . . my . . . my grandbaby was only fifteen."

The women gasped and a few went over to embrace her, offering comfort and solace.

"Please . . . please." She shrugged away from them unable to bear their touch.

This woman was seventy-three years old, and she had run to the church. She was running for

Jesus today. She just couldn't bear a human touch.

She needed to appeal to a power that could help her, in order to spare the rest of her grandchildren.

Hattie looked on silently. She knew the Lord's hand when she saw it. She would not interfere.

Gripping the cross that she had now pulled down from its place on the wall, she hiccupped. "Aw, Jesus, please, please . . . please, Lord! Please!"

Screaming in agony she said, "I'll do anything you want me to do, Lord. But please, please don't let them kill any more of my grandchildren. Oh, Jesus. Oh, please, Jesus!" She fell to her knees clutching the cross to her bosom.

28

The Summons

In the spiritual realm, the horn of a ram blew, *toot toot toot toot*. It was a call marshaling the angelic forces.

Sam stood next to Discernment, his head respectfully bowed. *Toot toot toot toot*. It was a summons. It was not just any summons; it was special because the Angelic Souls who were assembling all had one thing in common. In the flesh they had all been handicapped.

The handicaps ranged from blindness to deafness, as well as from Down's Syndrome to Alzheimer's. Each and every one had at one time carried some type of an affliction.

That was in flesh.

In spirit the Lord had cast his eyes upon them and not one affliction or handicap did he see. He had blessed them to be without a spot or a wrinkle, and then given them all the gift of *voice*.

He had looked past the deficiencies of the flesh and beheld the center core of their collective pureness of hearts. And all he saw was the beauty of their spirits.

As the Spirit of Discernment and the Spirit of Innocence looked on, the choir assembled in a holy procession, their robes pure white, their hearts singing one song, "Who Is the King of Glory?"

They stepped on the hallowed stairway on which they would stand singing for the next three days, until the exact hour that the Christ child had been born.

The first note soared through the heavens. Peace. Ah, Peace. Supreme, heavenly peace.

It was a lifting of the spirit.

A praise and worship service in the spirit, for the majesty of the Lord Jesus Christ that put the Spirit of Discernment and the little Spirit of Innocence on their knees with bowed heads.

The melody and lyrics soared higher as though eagles had been instructed to carry the sounds on their wings. And in the midst, the most powerful, awesome, and majestic Spirit resided. The Spirit of Spirits. The Spirit of the Amen, residing just as his spirit had once resided, on the face of the waters, on the face of the deep.

He saw all. He was all.

"God is not a man. God is a Spirit," the Spirit of Innocence said aloud.

The Spirit of Discernment put his arm around the little angel's shoulder.

"Yes, he is," the Spirit of Discernment agreed.

The notes, the singing, the jubilation for holiness, and the celebrations for the birth of Christ continued to soar around them.

The Spirit of Innocence looked down and saw people scrambling for their gift-wrapped purchases, running around stressing themselves out.

He also saw the depression on the ones who dreaded the Christmas season, and he felt a profound sadness that they had truly missed the whole point of Christmas.

None of the joy, jubilance, or peace of what Christ's birth was really about, could they feel or rejoice in. They had not embraced this concept of his birth.

"God is a Spirit! Don't you know?" the little Angel said as though they could hear him.

"He gave his only begotten son, so you could have life, and have it more abundantly. Don't you know?" Sam once again said to them. But, alas, they were deaf of ear. Ears that heard, and yet they did not hear.

Sam looked toward the altar. A tear came to his eye at what he was witnessing. The Lord Jesus Christ stood there looking down upon earth just as the Spirit of Innocence was doing.

The Spirit of Innocence marveled that he looked just like he did when he'd walked the earth, only there was a hallowed, holy light surrounding him. A luminescent glow that surrounded him in its pureness.

He marveled even more when he saw a teardrop sparkle in the eye of Christ, as he witnessed the people's actions on earth, and then stretched out his arms toward them, the holes of his crucifixion visible in his hands.

The teardrop finally slid from his eye. Blood dripped from his hands. Still it did not alter the actions, nor the behavior of the people on earth.

Sam felt a paralyzing sadness.

Discernment lifted his head up high, to stall a falling teardrop that was cascading down his own cheek, although it was in vain.

Jesus Christ truly was the forgotten spirit.

29

Every Man Has a Choice

"**E**very man has a choice," Bible Man stated emphatically from his position at the McDonald's roundtable.

Petey McWhorter snorted. He wasn't a regular but occasionally he joined in, adding his caustic remarks. "Ain't no choice, Bible Man. I ain't choose to be Black and poor, that just happened."

Darryl glanced over from his chess game, the hint of a smile touching his lips, as he waited for Bible Man's reply.

Bible Man thumped the cover of his Bible, as he was frequently known to do. "Fool, ain't nobody talking about that body you living in. I'm talking 'bout your spirit. You do have one you know."

"Yeah, well if I do," Petey retorted, "it ain't feeding me."

"You ain't feeding it," Bible Man replied.

Bible Man pushed the Bible toward Petey.

Petey angrily pushed it back. "Go 'head wit dat, man. You always gettin' mushy around Christmas time."

"Checkmate," Darryl said to his opponent, as he calmly stared at his position on the board. His opponent shook his head, slapping cash on the table, not bothering to argue about his defeat.

Bible Man who had been keeping an eye on the chess game, quickly tallied up an analogy. "See that's what I'm talking about, Petey. You done let the Devil checkmate you. Man he done stole your blessings."

Bible Man momentarily looked over at Darryl. "No offense man." Darryl was actually one of his favorite people.

"None taken," Darryl stated affectionately.

Some considered Bible Man odd. His code of dress was from the '60s. He was the only cat in Hartford still wearing bell-bottoms.

He was one heck of a walker for a man his age. He had to be sixty-nine if he was a day. He walked, and walked, and walked all over the city at all times of day and night. He was tireless.

When he wasn't walking he could be found in McDonald's talking, reading his Bible, and nursing the same cup of coffee all day.

Petey McWhorter rose from the table at the mention of the Devil, cuz he knew Bible Man could argue that point all day long. "Look here man. Ain't nobody stole nothing from me and ain't no devil backed me into no corner. I been in the corner since I entered the game from my mama's womb, and that's just word, man."

Bible Man leaned back, folding his arms across

his chest. He lost a bit of his fire while a pang of sorrow settled in his chest as he looked at Petey. "All I'm saying, Petey, is you got a choice," he said more softly.

He pointed to the Bible. "It's all in here, man. I'm telling you it is. In here is life. These words are living life. That's truth, man. Life like we ain't never knew it, Petey."

"Not for me it ain't," Petey said despondently, while leaving the restaurant.

"It's for anybody who wants it," Bible Man replied solemnly to the vacant space left by Petey.

"It's for anybody who wants it."

30

His Truth Is Marching On

Hattie sat down and wrote in her journal: *His truth is marching on . . .*

The refrain kept drumming in her head. *Glory Glory Hallelujah, Glory Glory Hallelujah.*

She continued her journaling as she thought of it, realizing that she would be leaving a road map to her feelings once she had gone on. And she knew that was fine. What needed to be said would be said.

She dipped her Waterford crystal pen into the inkwell, pursed her lips, and continued writing. She generally loved the images she conjured up, as she reflected on life's pieces from her own unique perspective.

But today she wasn't loving it because an unbidden image loomed.

There was a boiling sound similar to that of hot water on a stove when it reached the highest temperature, but it was being contained by the lid on the pot.

At any minute it could blow.

The sound got louder and then erupted, like the sound of a volcano. It was coming up through the city's sewers, seeping from underground. Like boiling, seething black lava, she could see it splashing down Albany Avenue all over the streets of Hartford.

Hattie knew in that instant the Spirit of Darkness was moving among their youth, causing them to destroy one another.

She set the journal down, praying in earnest.

That night Hattie dreamed she was at the pre-Christmas breakfast at George's house, when a stranger rang the doorbell. As he ascended the staircase she felt his presence, rather than saw him. Outside, blackbirds surrounded the house.

When she awoke she was shaking, so vivid was the dream. "Had to be a dream," she said aloud to herself.

The Spirit of Darkness

The Spirit of Darkness roamed the streets of Hartford, contemplating, evaluating, as well as assessing his next plan of action.

This was a timeless path for him. He'd been walking to and fro, caught in his own web of deception since before Christ.

Though he walked in their midst people were unable to see him. They actually could have seen, if they knew what to see, or even sensed him, if they'd had more belief, more faith, and if they weren't so caught up in only what they could see, feel, and touch.

This meant he was able to roam freely as there were precious few who had the sight, or the instincts, to know or trust that he was among them. The precious few who did know had always had great difficulty in convincing the others.

The Spirit of Darkness frowned as he thought of Jamie, a mere child who had caused him to lose one of his foot soldiers, the one at the train station who'd ended up frozen to death.

It was as it should be though, he considered, particularly if the idiot couldn't handle even a child.

He laughed aloud. *Good night, baby.*

He had rocked the rest of the spirit souls to sleep. On his part this was an extremely important achievement, because the placement of the soul's gifts among men, would spread goodwill and good cheer, and their gifts had the distinct ability to change a man's heart, or a woman's, or a child's, and so on and so forth, and that definitely could and would not be allowed, not as long as he was in existence. He was on the job. That is why they were all in eternal sleep.

He needed the hearts of people to be clouded in darkness. This was a vantage point from which he reached the highest pinnacle of evil.

He was sick with jealousy over this season that had been named for the Christ child each and every year.

Why didn't he have a season named after him?

After all he *was* Lucifer. He had at one time been God's right-hand man, before, well, before his fall from grace.

True, he had marshaled a takeover of God's kingdom that hadn't quite worked out, but still . . . well enough of that for now. He had other things to do, like pondering this Christmas thing.

He remembered back to the time of Herod when he had *almost* succeeded in altering the greatest plan in history.

He had entered Herod's spirit and told the Three Wise Men to bring him news of the birth of the holy child they sought, so that he himself might worship. Not! He had no such intention.

The Three Wise Men had betrayed him, and gone on their way after locating the child and leaving him gifts.

Yet he had still managed to learn their general destination, as well as the general area where it had been prophesied the child would be born.

He had slaughtered many of the male children under the age of two in that time and location, in order to ensure the death of the Holy child.

Incensed was too light a word to describe what he felt whenever this memory surfaced, because though he had slaughtered many, he'd been unable to touch one hair on the head of the Christ child. The child had escaped his grasp with his parents, Mary and Joseph.

So he'd been unable to alter history, and the child's effect on mankind with the power of his birth.

He'd wanted Christ's kingdoms, his glory, his fame, and his place in worship. He'd schemed to get it. He wanted it all. It should have been *his.*

He'd left heaven, well perhaps not left, but was tossed out, but nonetheless he'd left with a third of the angels, and should have been able to take over.

It really didn't matter. The point was he didn't want to stand by for another season of celebrating him whose name was the most spoken, as well as the most famous name in the world.

Christmas was in his name, and in his glory. Everything was about him. It was all about Jesus Christ, the Messiah, the Nazarene.

Jesus Christ laid down his life for the sheep, he mimicked to himself. He didn't know how many times he'd heard those words.

Too many was what he did know.

He could never fathom why Christ had bothered to die, and be crucified on a cross for so many who essentially showed no respect. It couldn't have been him. It would have been off with their heads, no tender mercy, and mild, here.

He'd actually had a hand in instigating Christ's death, but it had backfired on him, and ended up only to the glory of Christ. God's plan had been untouchable, as well as one that could not be altered.

He was no longer walking. He'd become so angered with this particular memory that he was sweeping through the streets, among the people now, as he traveled down memory lane. The road less traveled.

Calming himself, he knew he'd managed to muddy the waters though, so that people had gotten away from solely worshipping Jesus Christ at Christmas.

He was proud of this particular deception, because unknowingly to the people, this selective brand of deception had caused a lot of pain in the spirit. In his slyness he'd managed to make a lot of them forget about Jesus.

Warming to this part of the memory he slowed to a walk once again, as he thought about how he had scattered the thoughts of the people like sheep to the wind. He'd separated them like sheep from, and without, their shepherd. He laughed.

Right now he was working on making some of the books in man's world have more notoriety so it would confuse the masses.

He'd had them sell millions around the world just to grab the people's attention. He'd even managed to suggest that Christ was a mere human.

And now there was book after book exploring Christ's lineage. That was a real power move there. He congratulated himself. There were even people claiming to be blood related to him. Shoot, when he thought about it, he was better than he'd given himself credit for.

Anyway regarding the scattering of the sheep, he'd managed in the process to sow seeds of doubt in their worldly little minds. Not all of them still believed.

Some ran around from shopping mall to shopping mall, store to store, completely skewed on what the Christmas season was really about, in hunt for the physical, with not a thought for the spiritual.

He had also infiltrated the religions of man, teaching them to believe more in the education of religion, than in the spirit of God. He'd managed to sow pure folly among them.

That was why they had lost the key of knowledge, unbeknownst to them. Because they thought they were smarter, and wanted to rely on their own intellect.

Who needed spirit when one had intelligence?

But still there were some diehards. Right here in the city of Hartford, there was one smart-mouthed child, who thought she could spread the love of Christ, without obstacle or difficulty.

He turned the corner to her street. He stood watching her house. He focused in on her bedroom window, as he listened to the noise of some knuckle-headed boys playing touch football in the street.

Why couldn't she have been more like them?

All they wanted was some shiny gifts under the Christmas tree, and a few envelopes of green stuff. They wouldn't even say a prayer in acknowledgment of the Christ Child on Christmas Day. Yay!

But *no*, Jamie had to feel her job was to spread love, share goodness with everyone with whom she came in to contact. She aspired to be a direct worker for the Lord Jesus Christ.

The instant her great-grandmother, the old bag, had mentioned Jesus to her, she had been set on a course of no return, the fire for Christ lit in her heart. He suspected she'd been born to that cause.

Before it was all over he'd see about changing her course, dousing her fire, and perhaps ridding the world of her entirely.

That night he entered her dreams, as she lay sleeping, disguised as one of the many images of Christ that had been put forth, before the world.

As he sat next to her, happy in his deceit because he had gotten so close to her, she looked over at him, briefly. She asked, "Are you without sin?"

The heavens sang at her question. She waited innocently for his answer.

He was so startled that he hesitated a fraction of a second too long. In that instant she knew, and he was stripped of his disguise.

Jamie merely smiled sadly at him before he dissipated. Once again the child had defeated him.

The Stardust Angel

High up in the sky, in the beauty of twilight, when night was like smooth black velvet, and the stars were like a lighted path to heaven there stood an angel, poised on her tiptoes, awaiting the first chord of music.

When it reached her ears, she twirled once, twice, and then once again, full circle. She was dancing on a star. Praise and worship in dance form. She flailed her arms, shook her head, touched her heart, and offered up the highest of praises to God Almighty and his son Jesus Christ.

She danced, danced, danced, legs kicking, perfect twirls, her head thrown back, caught in the spirit of worship without restraint. Her fingers spread wide, outstretching to their full length, light cascaded across the sky as though her very fingers were lit batons, lighting streaks leading to heaven.

She jumped high in the sky, putting her agility, on full splendid display, demonstrating poise, humility, and grace, in a single stroke.

Sweat appeared on her brow. Her eyes were shut tight. She could hear nothing but the chords of the music she danced to.

She could see nothing but the silver light behind her eyelids.

She could smell nothing except holiness in the air.

She could feel nothing except the wind beneath her feet.

She could touch nothing except the creation of air.

She stopped on a dime atop the star.

She then spread her arms wide, threw her head back in a perfect arc, she twirled one last time, her expression a reflection of humbleness.

Her hair was as black as midnight, and as thick as linen. It was set in thick cornrows that formed a crown around her head. Her hair glistened with stardust. Her brow sparkled with the crystalline effect of her own sweat.

Finally she spoke. "Hallelujah! All praise be to the Christ child! Let *every* thing that has breath worship him!"

She bowed her head; gracefully she slipped down on one knee, on top of the star. Her head tilted toward heaven. Her eye was on the prize.

The star glittered over the earth. It moved a little closer carrying the Angel girl. The Stardust Angel remained in her position of praise.

Once again the highest praise slipped from

between her lips, "Hallelujah!" The sound of the word leaving her mouth reverberated throughout the atmosphere.

"Hallelujah!"

The highest of praises was carried on home.

George and Georgette Brooks

George and Georgette's lives had been intricately entwined since they emerged from Beatrice's womb twenty-two years ago. George was older by a mere three minutes.

Even on that sunny day as they were thrust into the harsh light of the world, their tiny fingers had reached for one another's. It was a bond that even their own mother couldn't break.

Since the very day they were born they were without doubt the darlings of the Brooks clan. Beatrice treated them like twin Barbie dolls.

George was a bit more aggressive than Georgette; Georgette disliked things but her response to them was rarely verbal.

In a natural progression, because they always gravitated toward each other, it stood to reason when one stumbled down a path of darkness, the other twin was sure to go as well.

G-Tang may have been Beatrice's only focus, but he was certainly not her only problem. The twins were skirting various realms as well. She would have discovered that if she had paid her informant to look further than G-Tang, when it came to matters of the streets.

Beatrice hadn't felt any particular attachment to the twin's daddy, so consequently she didn't yearn to see their artfully drawn features, as she did with G-Tang.

However, she was never one to miss a shot to flaunt her worth, so she had constantly kept her beautiful twins on stage in one way or another, all of their lives, and the twins had grown accustomed to both the stage and the attention.

As they reached adulthood they were still looking to dance and prance on that same stage, only they ended up searching and finding it in the magic of darkness.

We all fall down.

In a converted warehouse on the south end of Hartford, in an exclusive, very private members-only club the twins discovered the occult, sex, and drugs, all in that order, and had entered a world many times removed from their lives on the surface.

As well it was many times removed from the foundation of Christianity.

They were models of decorum where careers and family were concerned. But at night the wolves came out to play, and George and Georgette were tasty fresh morsels laid out, on a platter of depravation, degradation, and the hidden world existing within great darkness. The world they entered was splattered with evil.

This particular night as each twin changed into the black hooded attire in which they worshipped, they each found themselves staring with wide eyes in the mirror of their own reflection.

Georgette blinked as she recalled the pre-Christmas breakfast dream. She'd had it once again, as she had come to call it. She'd never had the dream before that breakfast, she was certain.

She'd not been able to shake the dream, nor the presence attached to it, though she didn't know why. There was a disturbing individual in their midst but she didn't know who he was or why he was there.

George was experiencing identical circumstances in his dressing room, which was attached to Georgette's.

Georgette and George each frowned as they looked down at the Holy Bible, with a pair of Black hands folded on top of it.

Never had either of them seen that before, and they certainly wouldn't have seen it, given their present circumstances, under any condition, nor by any stretch of the imagination.

Georgette lifted her head to peer once again in the mirror, and the blackness of her existence stared back, challenging her.

Her twin had done the same thing at the exact moment, in his dressing room, making the same identical discovery.

Without warning each Bible flipped open, but instead of the text written on the pages, the book flashed scenes of their Christmases past.

Encompassed in those scenes were love, warmth, and memories, as well as snippets of the Gospel shared by their grandmother Hattie.

They were thrust into the animation of their collective past.

The book closed of its own accord, just the same as it had opened. The twins were stricken by the act. Disbelieving expressions registered on their faces, altering their features.

Almost hypnotically they each reached the door to their adjoining dressing rooms at the same time.

Dealing in black magic they had each become accustomed to out-of-the-ordinary circumstances, but for some reason this very act in itself had shaken them to their core.

George snatched the door open a mere second before Georgette. She was standing there on the other side of the door, just as he had known she would be.

"I want to go back." She uttered the words before he could make one sound.

"I want to go back where I came from, back to the light. I can't stay in this darkness," she said. Her bottom lip trembled from the force of what she was saying.

George assessed his twin, and then nodded his agreement. "I know."

If they didn't get out they would die. Of that there was no doubt. They would be dead of spirit, stripped of their life forces. They saw it all in the split of a second.

A knife slashed, blood splashed, and George and Georgette stood on the fringes of black magic, at the point of no return. This was their last chance.

In a flash they realized they had made a mistake fighting so hard to dance on that stage in front of an audience, any audience.

They each heard the strains of "The First Noel." Its lyrics and melody drifted mildly into their ears, the lyrics lulling them, "The Angel did say!"

The Stardust Angel rose from bended knee, continuing to dance on her star. It was okay to be on stage, it just had to be the right stage.

Then a strange occurrence happened. For the first time since he'd entered eternal sleep, the Soul of Love turned in his sleep. It must be duly noted that Love had never before, not even once, moved.

Jamie dreamed.

In her dream she reached out her hands to George and Georgette, who she now realized were hanging from the edge of a cliff, with nothing but the sky above them and the depths of rocks and water, far, far below.

With all the strength she could muster, she stretched her fingers until she could reach each of them with one hand. She looked into their tear-drenched eyes, and smiled.

They each grabbed a hand instinctively knowing that if they could latch onto her, they would be saved from the dark abyss awaiting them.

Once she had a firm grip on them she hauled them on top of the cliff to safety.

We all fall down.

Drained from the physical exertion of her dream,

the little girl made the world-weariest sound in her sleep that Sam had ever heard.

"She is merely tired, Sam," Discernment said.

Protectively Sam wiped the sweat from her brow. But, their greatest battle was soon to begin.

34

Being a Child

"Jamie!" Cydney yelled from her front yard, as Jamie descended the steps from her porch. "Jamie, come over here!" She beckoned excitedly.

After a breakfast where Jamie had stuffed herself on her Grandma Lizzie's strawberry French toast, she was slow moving.

Her grandmother had spread strawberry marmalade all over the French toast, just as she knew Jamie liked it. Unable to help herself she had managed to stuff three slices of it, plus ham and eggs, into her mouth.

Now she was paying the price as she looked next door to see Cydney jumping up and down at her appearance.

Cydney and she had lived next door to each other all of their lives. They were best friends, as well as the same age.

In fact the following day Cydney would be a guest at Grandma Lizzie's breakfast table, just as she was every year, the day before Christmas Eve.

"Do you want to jump rope?" Cydney asked as Jamie plopped herself on the front steps.

"I don't think so," Jamie said with the pained expression of one who has overeaten.

Cydney grinned. "You just came from the breakfast table. Didn't you?"

Jamie only nodded placing a hand over her stomach. Then they both burst out laughing.

"Don't worry. Tomorrow we can be full together," Cydney said, barely able to wait for her turn to sit down at Mrs. Lizzie's sumptuous breakfast table.

Jamie sat forward on the step sniffing the air. "What's that smell?"

Cydney shook her head in annoyance wrinkling her nose. "You know that's old man, oops," she caught herself remembering to address all adults respectfully, "You know that's Mr. Barlow roasting his chestnuts on the open fire, or more likely burning them like he do every year," Cydney finished with a giggle.

Jamie jumped up from the step and grabbed Cydney's hand. "Come on, let's go watch."

Jamie was fascinated with Old Man Barlow, as many called him. He was G-Tang's granddaddy, and that made her even more interested in him. He didn't seem to have much of a relationship with G-Tang, but still, he was his granddaddy, so that made him like family in Jamie's eyes.

They raced to Mr. Barlow's backyard, where just as predicted he was indeed roasting chestnuts.

He smiled at the two girls, two of his favorite

kids in the neighborhood. He had purposely
brought marshmallows in case they were outside
and lured by the smell of roasting chestnuts. And,
here they both were. Mission accomplished.

"Well, good morning, beautiful ladies!" he
greeted them.

"Good morning, Mr. Barlow," they chirped in
unison.

"Care for any breakfast?" He had bacon grilling
on the side.

Jamie grimaced. Cydney shook her head no.

"Suit yourselves. How about a roasted marshmallow?"

To this they both agreed. When they were
ready he handed one to each of them.

Mr. Barlow sniffed the air. "Well too bad, we're
not going to have a white Christmas. There isn't
going to be any snow. I guess we'll just be looking at these drab gray concrete streets."

Jamie and Cydney finished the marshmallows
in record speed and began to play a hand game
that Cydney's mother had taught them, from
her own childhood.

Jamie laughed while keeping her focus on
the hand clapping she and Cydney were doing.
It was one of her favorite games. She also liked
the rhythm of the hand clapping because the
words rhymed.

*Oh Mary Mack Mack Mack, all dressed in black,
black, black.* She chanted the words silently in
her head now instead of out loud, because they
were talking to Mr. Barlow.

"Don't worry, Mr. Barlow," Jamie said, not missing a beat. "We're going to have a white Christmas. There's going to be a whole ton of snow."

Mr. Barlow sniffed the air again, while turning a burnt chestnut. This little chestnut burning ritual was strictly to put him in the mood for Christmas, nothing else.

"'Fraid not," he said. "My nose ain't never let me down, and I don't expect it to do so now. There's no snow in the air for this Christmas. That's for sure."

Jamie shook her head in the negative. "Okay, Mr. Barlow. You'll see."

"Girl this nose of mine is near 'bout seventy-seven years old. I'd know if there were snow in the air."

"Mr. Barlow, do you know what a miracle is?" Jamie suddenly asked, not breaking her patty-cake rhythm with Cydney, and still reciting the poetry to the game in her head.

Mr. Barlow stopped in the middle of roasting another marshmallow. "Of course I do, young lady. But let me hear your version of a miracle."

"A miracle is when you don't believe something will happen, but it will anyway."

Old Man Barlow smiled. He couldn't help himself. "And, when did you get to be so smart?"

Jamie frowned seriously contemplating the question.

She answered, for the first time halting the patty-cake game. "I only got to be smart when I learned about Jesus."

Old Man Barlow was startled by her answer.

"He's the reason for the season, you know. He's also the reason we'll have snow. He's gonna pour down tons of it, nice and white and fluffy, cuz he knows we want it. Besides I asked him special for it along with my biggest request."

"And that is?" Mr. Barlow questioned.

Jamie cast her eyes downward. Her long lashes hid her pain. For an instant she reminded Old Man Barlow of his grandson G-Tang, whom he longed to see more of. The long fringed lashes were one of the Brooks family traits.

"For my mommy to come home for Christmas."

Mr. Barlow couldn't believe anyone had filled this precious child's head with this nonsense. He knew her mother was incarcerated in a federal prison, and there was no way she'd be home for Christmas.

Jamie's answer had rendered him speechless. He actually tried to speak to rid her mind of this nonsense, and found himself mute.

Cydney put an arm around her friend's shoulders sensing the tears she couldn't see. One of them escaped Jamie's eyes, splattering on Cydney's shoe. Cydney pulled her closer, trying to shield her from the pain.

Mr. Barlow patted the top of Jamie's head, his roasting of the chestnuts forgotten.

The Spirit of Darkness stood on the edge of Old Man Barlow's property trying to restore Barlow's speech so he could taint this child's faith of miracles, before realizing that special powers had once again stepped in to assist the child, and that he could not alter it.

He watched another tear drop from her eye.

He knew it wouldn't be the last one she shed, before he got through with her.

35

The Haunting of the Music

G-Tang had just finished slapping together a peanut butter and jelly sandwich, trying to abate his munchies, when he first heard it.

Initially, he dismissed the sound thinking Beatrice was pulling a prank to get his attention. He ignored the music, intent on slathering as much strawberry jam as he could get on his sandwich. Prior to the making of this sandwich he had washed down a bag of Famous Amos's chocolate chip cookies, with a quart of milk.

He stopped to pay attention as he heard—again—Michael Jackson singing, "I Saw Mommy Kissing Santa Claus." The same song his dad used to dance to, with him, and his mother at Christmas time.

He listened intently, laying the sandwich down. His hunger had gone the way of the wind, his sugar craving an instant thing of the past.

He walked slowly toward the door that led to

the attic. G-Tang was positive he heard the song now, no doubt. He ascended the steps to the attic like a sleepwalker.

He could hear the music clearly, both the melody and lyrics, just as clearly as he had heard them when his father danced with him and his mother, holding them close.

Reaching the top stair he hesitated. There was a chill in the air, which caused him to rub his arms.

The music was growing louder. Feeling a bit spooked, G-Tang chided himself on the paranoid effects of smoking too much weed. Maybe he should quit.

Staring at the CD player, he knew the music *was* playing, but the CD player was turned off. G-Tang pulled the plug from the wall but the music didn't stop. In fact the song was blaring from the speakers.

He took one step back and found himself face to face with the past once again, watching his father hold him and Beatrice, while dancing to "I Saw Mommy Kissing Santa Claus."

His father winked.

"G-Tang," he said looking at him as he was now, at seventeen, while still holding him in his arms, as he had been as a child.

"I found out the love of Christ exists. Reach for it, son."

He reached out a hand touching G-Tang's heart. "Believe that. It's right here. There's a better road for you than there was for me, son. Don't follow the streets as I did."

G-Tang stared at his father, speechless. It was all so very real.

That night G-Tang's daddy would be found dead of massive heart failure. His dying wish had been that he would be able to hold his son, as he used to, one last time for Christmas. His last words were, "Jesus, remember me."

36

The Confession

Sharese stood in the Wadsworth Atheneum museum in downtown Hartford staring up at one of its precious acquisitions of art.

She really wasn't up for this clandestine meeting with Dwayne, and she still had many things to do in preparation for Christmas. But, Dwayne was her brother so she would give him an audience to hear him out.

She had decided for the first time in many years to attend a Christmas Eve church service. Generally she spent Christmas Eve drinking and dancing, at least after her ritual family appearance at Uncle George's house.

But this Christmas the pull was strong for her to attend a church service. Though it wouldn't be her grandmother Hattie's church.

She loved her grandmother dearly and considered her a treasure in her own right, but there would be too much pressure if she were to attend her grandmother's church.

The people there would fawn over her, and she'd have to show a high degree of tolerance, because her grandmother was also one of the founding members, so her entire demeanor would be scrutinized.

Attending service there would mean she'd also have to wear her chief financial officer title. She'd have to wear it like a trophy you put on the mantel. They'd be pleased with her accomplishments, and they'd wear them as if they were their own accomplishments.

She didn't want adoration; she wanted some peace in her spirit. She needed to attend a church that would allow her to glide in unnoticed, and unknown, where she could park herself in the back pew, waiting.

Waiting for what she didn't quite know. But, she would wait for something, anything that would remove her pain.

Dwayne arrived looking as handsome as ever, dressed in one of Stackpole Moore Tryon's most expensively tailored signature suits. He brushed a kiss on her cheek, leaving a whiff of his Italian cologne in his wake.

In the quiet of the museum, close to Sharese's ear, he made his confession, clearing his soul as though Sharese herself were a spiritual confessional.

Sharese couldn't believe her ears. The relationship he spoke of made her heart flutter. She couldn't believe how unaware she'd been. She must have seen it a thousand times, but not *seen* it.

Her own brother, her very own flesh and blood, had managed to penetrate a crack in the very existence of her foundation, or at least of what she perceived it to be.

She couldn't believe Dwayne had breached in such a tumultuous way the boundaries of her life. His confession was explosive, and could very well blow up in all of their faces, particularly hers, destroying her financially, as well as socially.

While Dwayne was feeling cleansed after his confession, Sharese, the one person in the world whom he thought would understand, was feeling blood raging in her heart.

She turned on her $400 pumps, and said, "The next time you need a confessional, Dwayne, use a church."

She slapped his face so hard and soundly the echo reverberated throughout the museum. The imprint of her hand rested on his cheek.

The last thing he heard were her heels clicking on the floor, walking away from him.

37

A Touch of Evil

Jamie sat cross-legged with her chin in her hands staring listlessly at the brightly lit Christmas tree. She saw it, yet she didn't see it.

George puffed on his pipe, listening to the fire crackle. From time to time he cast sideways glances in his granddaughter's direction. He'd already started and stopped several times on his way to conversation with her.

He couldn't bear the pain emanating from his baby girl. In past years she'd sat in that same position with joy etched into her features, as well as laughter bubbling up from her lips, as she tried to guess what was in each beautifully wrapped package.

He feared the pain of Cynthia's absence was getting to be too much for her to bear. He questioned his wisdom in telling her emphatically that her mother wouldn't be home for Christmas.

Lizzie had, of course, cautioned him against doing just that. However, he couldn't have allowed Christmas to just arrive with no Cynthia, because that pain might have caused her even greater emotional harm.

He sighed.

Lizzie cast concerned glances Jamie's way as well, because she had picked through her favorite dinner of lasagna.

Jamie was aware of their glances but she was tired inside, so very tired. She had never been so tired before. Also, her body was filled with a heat she'd never felt before. It felt like a furnace was burning inside of her.

She was having difficulty keeping her eyes open. Her eyelids felt very heavy, like weights. In addition her insides were quivering. Her tongue was growing thick in her mouth.

She reached over to click on the musical lights, without much enthusiasm. "The First Noel" lit the tree, and the room, with its melodic spirit and sound.

Jamie heard her grandmother's voice clearly saying, "No matter how hard it gets or what anyone says, Jamie, you've got to believe."

She didn't know why grandma was saying that again. She'd already said that to her. In any case those were the last words she heard as she curled up on the floor near the tree, falling into a deep lethargic sleep.

She looked so peaceful that it would be an hour or so before George and Lizzie had the heart to awaken her.

She looked like a sleeping, peaceful, little

angel curled up under the tree in her new patch-work, red and green, Christmas pajamas.

Jamie was anything but peaceful. A high-grade fever was raging through her body. She was in a battle for her life.

She couldn't have moved if she had wanted to. Which she didn't because she could no longer stand the pain of her own existence, which was why she had fallen into a deep sleep.

Lizzie went over to touch her brow, only to find her skin raging hot to the touch.

Jamie's cheeks were an unnatural candy apple red. They were downright splotchy with spots of heat.

"Oh my God," she mumbled.

George hearing the stricken tone lacing her voice raised his voice, much louder than his usual tone. "What, Lizzie?" he asked, his voice reflecting exasperation instead of the concern he was feeling.

"George, Jamie is burning up. I don't mean just hot. I mean burning up."

Jamie's skin was now covered in a sleek sheen of glistening wetness. She wasn't moving. She wouldn't even open her eyes at Lizzie's probing. She lay there, not stirring.

George raced over to touch his granddaughter. He'd barely touched her and his fingers had been scorched, as though he'd stuck them in a raging fire.

Without hesitation George scooped Jamie up in his arms, running for the door.

"Where are you going, George?" Lizzie yelled startled by his actions, and unable to think clearly.

"To the hospital."

"Don't you want me to call 911?"

"No. They're not quick enough. I'll get her there faster. Grab the cell phone; call all of the family on the way. Send the car for Mama. Let's go."

By this time George was already at the front door, with Jamie in his arms. Lizzie grabbed the phone.

A startling sight met George when he pulled open his front door.

Blackbirds.

Every inch of his yard was covered with them. They stood very still; at attention watching him put Jamie in the car.

Lizzie saw them too.

She jumped in the backseat with Jamie. She pulled her grandbaby close to her body, cradling her.

"George, what are all those birds doing in our yard?"

"I don't know," George responded as he gunned the car out of the driveway, thinking the birds would fly away at the sound, but instead they stood their ground.

For some odd reason George found that strangely comforting.

He would have found it even more comforting, had he known more about the touch of evil, the hand that had touched his granddaughter, locking her into a seal of death.

38

Family

Lizzie was one of the calmest people in the Brooks family, so when her calls of distress went out, it struck chords of panic.

Naturally the first call she placed was to her mother-in-law, Hattie. Valiantly she tried to abate the panic from her voice, but one thing Hattie was good at, was reading people.

The instant she heard Lizzie's voice a chord of fear struck her. There was something in the timbre of her voice, combined with the fact that she couldn't shake a song she'd been hearing for days.

> *Wading in the water.*
> *Wading in the wat-wat-wat-er.*
> *Wading in the water.*
> *Hmmm, hmmm, hmmm, in the water.*

"Hattie," Lizzie hesitated, not wanting to shock the old woman. She knew Hattie was strong, and had a will like iron. But she also knew this child bundled in the backseat of the car with a raging fever, the likes of which she'd never seen, with her eyes closed, whose brow she kept wiping while placing the calls, was the center of Hattie's world.

"Hattie . . . Jamie."

A chill shot through Hattie at the mere mention of Jamie's name, along with that cautious tone Lizzie was using on her.

Hattie closed her eyes. She saw a creek. In a voice that belied her panic she asked, "What about my Jamie?"

"She . . . She . . . ," Lizzie's voice broke. Tears streamed down her face.

Panic stricken Hattie opened her eyes. The creek was still there. She yelled into the phone. "She what?"

Softly Lizzie said, "She won't open her eyes. George and I are in the car. We're taking her to St. Francis Hospital."

Calmly Hattie said, "Hang up the phone. Call my car, Lizzie."

The next thing Lizzie heard was the dial tone. She called the car to pick Hattie up.

Next she called Beatrice. She really wanted to call Sharese because Jamie was like the light of her world, but she didn't want to break family protocol.

It saddened her that she couldn't call her daughter, Jamie's mother, and be instantly connected, but later she would place an emergency call to the prison.

Beatrice's slurred voice slid over the line into her ear. Realizing the call was being placed from her brother's cell phone, which he in fact never used, she became more alert.

She raised her voice an octave. For a moment she sounded like her mother's daughter. "What?"

Lizzie brought her up to speed on the situation.

"Okay. David and I will be there. We're on our way." She hung up hitting the house intercom button.

"David!"

G-Tang jumped. He was about to make a smart remark when he noticed sadness in her voice.

"David we have to go to St. Francis Hospital. They can't wake Jamie up," her voice ended on a soft note.

G-Tang frowned. His heart thumped. "What?"

"Let's go, David!" Beatrice's voice was strong, demanding again. He jumped out of bed, climbing into his jeans, and Timbs.

As much as that little girl got on his nerves, he certainly didn't want her to die. Instinctively he sensed she was near death. And, he'd never heard of a child who couldn't be awakened.

Why couldn't Jamie open her eyes?

G-Tang threw his jacket on, and headed to the door. For the first time in his natural born life, he prayed.

Sharese sat holding her head between her hands, immobile. She'd received Lizzie's call. Between Dwayne's confession, and the peril of her most beloved family member, her life was spiraling out of control.

Jamie had the purest heart in her family. She had so much love to share. Why couldn't she open her eyes?

Uncharacteristically, she called a cab. She couldn't concentrate nor summon the energy to drive her own car.

She sat in the back of the cab, staring vacantly out of the window. What was happening to her life? And, why couldn't Jamie open her eyes? She heard both questions for the one-hundredth time. What she didn't hear was the answer.

The twins had been paged from a late dinner they were sharing while contemplating the extraordinary circumstance of their own lives. They rode side by side in the car service in silence, locked into their own thoughts of what the family would be like if its light and center, Jamie, died.

Dwayne, after receiving the call, simply put his hands on top of the old black, wizened ones on the Bible he'd too discovered as had his twin siblings, and prayed hard for the love and brightness to not be dampened or shut off in this precious little girl.

Meanwhile, Cynthia was pacing her cell.

She didn't know why, but she was. Something was terribly wrong. She could feel it. Something was out of kilter.

And, the most disturbing thing of all, she realized during her pacing was that she could no longer hear the dripping of the water.

Drip. Drip. Drip. It was no more. In its place was nothing, but silence.

"Please, Lord. What's the matter?" she asked.

"Jamie," she whispered through no will of her own. Panicked she turned around. Her eyes were automatically transfixed on the picture of her child.

She didn't know how but she was now certain, beyond a shadow of a doubt, that something was wrong. Her voice caught on a sob, as she yelled, "Guard!"

She grabbed a book she'd been reading, banging on the bars. "Guard!"

"Oh, my God! Please God keep my baby safe. Please. I promise I'll change my ways if you just keep her."

"Please, Lord!" Cynthia's voice had risen to screeching heights, as fear shook her entire body.

"Oh, please, God! Please." On the last note she spoke the entire prison went black. The prison was plunged into darkness, into the first blackout it had ever experienced.

The blackout threw the prison into chaos. A silly thought ran through Cynthia's mind.

The night the lights went out in Georgia.

Then she dropped to her knees praying the most heartfelt prayer of her life.

"Create in me a pure heart, Oh, God, and renew a steadfast spirit within me." She repeated the words, not knowing how she remembered them. She had heard them long ago from the Book of Psalms.

There'd never been a man who prayed and

praised the Lord like David, the author of the Book of Psalms.

He had left a legacy in spirit for those who wished to reach out to the spirit of the Lord.

Cynthia reached for his words in the spirit.

39

12:01 A.M.
The Day Before Christmas
Eve

At 12:01 A.M., one minute past midnight, Hattie decided she'd had enough of the hospital's antics, as well as their lack of effectiveness, where her great-granddaughter's life was concerned.

She knew the doctors were trying and giving it their best, but their medical best wasn't good enough.

Jamie's body couldn't sustain those temperatures or afflictions for very much longer.

Hattie didn't know what she was going to do, but she knew it would be something. Drastic times called for drastic measures.

Against the doctor's orders to stay away, she leaned heavily on her cane and limped toward the emergency room, where Jamie was being treated.

"Lord, give me strength," she uttered on her way.

George watched his mother with her head tilted at the angle that said the only mind she was following was her own. He knew it would be useless to remind her of the hospital's orders of no family being allowed, only emergency medical personnel in the area where Jamie was being monitored.

Hattie limped to Jamie's side, as though she were being housed in her own home. The Lord didn't say stay away, so it wasn't so, as far as Hattie was concerned.

Discernment gave a small smile upon seeing her.

Sam wailed louder, without breaking stride. He had been at that high-pitched piercing wail ever since Jamie hadn't awakened.

Hattie stopped for a moment and stared directly at the two angels. Her eyes were wide open. She wanted to comfort the little one, but there was no time. Besides, they needed every battle cry in the spirit they could get. Sam's wounded spirit had the ability to get attention from exactly where they needed it. Heaven.

She looked at the elder Angel, who, knowing what answer she was seeking, shook his head briefly in the negative. They could not intervene.

Still she was comforted by their loyalty, as well as their presence.

Deep inside Hattie had known they couldn't help. If they could have helped in any way, this wouldn't have been carried out this far. If they had had the power to prevent it, they would have.

The old woman nodded her understanding. She wiped a tear from her eye.

When she stepped to the bedrail and witnessed her great-granddaughter's abused body, that one tear became a flood.

She clearly understood why the hospital wanted the family kept out. Every inch of the child's body was covered in bloodred blotches, and she was burning hot to the touch.

Hattie prayed hard. This wasn't the time for tears and weakness.

"Dear Lord, if you'd just hear me now!" The creek she'd been seeing overflowed. It rose up beyond the normal water level, spilling out onto the land.

Wading in the water. The song grew loud in her ears, as though someone were blasting a stereo system. The water in the creek washed up on the rocks now, with great power and force. The magnitude of it caught Hattie's attention.

She gasped. The water was no longer crystal clear, as it had been when she was a child. The water was blood red. The creek river was running red.

Wading in the water. She heard the lyrics again. The high decibel of the song increased in volume, as well as in intensity. In an insightful flash, Hattie suddenly knew what must be done.

The tears dried.

Her purpose returned. She was so happy that she temporarily lost her limp. She strode with purpose toward her son, but not before she whispered to her great-granddaughter, "Hang on baby. Everything is going to be all right. Jesus Christ is still on his throne."

George sat bolt upright in his chair when he saw the purposeful stride of his mother.

Hattie's appearance was so electric that the entire Brooks clan focused on her. Every eye in the room was on her as she approached George, whispering in his ear.

Her demand startled him, shaking him down to his very bones. His mother was a bold woman, but with this demand she would top even herself. Yet as outrageous as it seemed, it never, not even once, occurred to him to refuse her.

He stood up. "Lizzie give Mama the cell phone. Dwayne and David come with me to the men's room." George was left to look after the women.

Hattie left the presence of the rest of the family. She placed one very important call.

40

The Second Miracle

The doors to Hattie's church had been thrown wide open. So had the doors to the baptismal pool.

Hattie had been a supportive member of the church for forty years. She was one of the founding members back when there'd been only the preacher and ten members.

She used to tarry for the Lord's blessings, on her knees on a hard floor in front of a folding chair. Tarrying in those days had been considered the equivalent of praying as well as seeking favor with the Lord.

She'd never asked for even one favor in her forty years of service.

But, tonight was different. A child's life was at stake. As far as she was concerned it was time for people to put their faith and belief where their mouths were.

She knew everything was possible for those

who believed. She was a staunch believer in the
Lord Jesus Christ. She had witnessed his hand,
as well as his spirit on many an occasion.

The following day would be Christmas Eve.
She was determined her family would not be
spending it in a hospital in a death vigil for a
child who had yet to live, nevertheless to die.

So, after forty years, she had called in her
marker. She had made a call for a donation of
spirit to her life and that of her family. All of the
members of the church who needed to be in attendance were. Not one of them was missing.

The minister of the church, his wife, as well
as the two assistant ministers were all in attendance.

The choir was finely arrayed in their robes,
ready to marshal their voices as one to send up
praise and worship in the spirit. Although they
sang every Sunday, they had never sung to the
purpose they had now. They had been touched
in their very spirits, before one note had even
left their mouths.

Discernment had to grin at the picture that
was being laid out before him. Hattie was something else when it came to the Lord Jesus
Christ. Even Sam with his red-rimmed eyes had
stopped howling in anticipation of what he felt
in the air.

He was sitting quietly by Discernment. And,
for the first time in his angelic life span, he was
totally silent. There was no fidgeting, no jumping up and down, and no stumbling. He sat in
anticipation with everyone else.

The choir stood at the front doors of the
church ready to march down the aisle in praise.

All the ministers, as well as the elders surrounded the baptismal pool.

It was a sight to see. It was even more of a sight to feel, to watch these men humbled in their cause, standing by that baptismal pool, in one spirit and of one mind.

It was something that had always been a difficult achievement, for people to be of one frame of mind, but this was an extraordinary day.

Private security guards had been posted on the street, as well as on all of the blocks leading up to, and around the church. They totally surrounded the church. Additional guards had been posted directly in front of the church, leading right up to the church's doors.

The Hartford police and the chief, a black woman who had been minded by Hattie when she was a child, had been apprised of the situation.

Markers and favors had been called in. I.O.U.s had been exchanged, all in the honor of unity.

Hattie's family members were the only private citizens, so to speak, in attendance at the church, outside of the clergy members and choir.

By this time it was 3 A.M.

George, Dwayne, and David were missing from the front pews, where the family was congregated. Only George sitting next to his twin Georgette, who had caught a sudden case of *The Omen*–like shivers as she entered the church, was left of the males in the family sitting with the women.

He had been the male designated to keep an eye on the women in the family in case they needed some male support.

There was a presence in the air. George was downright scared.

He glanced at Georgette, whose fear was palpable. Her eyes were ovals of gray. They were stretched as wide open as possible with unmistakable fright.

His own eyes were a startling shade of jade, he would have discovered if he could have seen them.

Sharese sat primly, her legs crossed at the ankles, twisting a well-used handkerchief in her hand, dabbing at her swollen, red, tear-stained eyes.

Beatrice had never been as sober or as wide-awake as she was now. Immediately after hearing the news about Jamie, she had learned of Chance Barlow's death.

When it rains it pours and it certainly was pouring in Beatrice's life, as she walked down memory lane recalling every second spent with the greatest love of her life, Chance Barlow.

A part of her had died, when she heard the news.

She'd harbored a secret wish that he might one day be released. Now the last hope of that was gone. It had been spirited away in the blink of an eye, when Chance's spirit separated from his body.

Unthinkingly, she reached over and took Sharese's handkerchief. Sharese who was sitting next to her was startled. She swallowed her angry retort when she realized her tough, get-down-in-a-brawl-in-a-New-York-minute mother was crying.

For as long as she'd been born Sharese had never, ever seen her mother cry.

The twins looked startled by this turn of events, as well. Sharese put her arm around her mother, stroking her arm, pulling her close. It was a gesture she had not practiced with her mother much over the years.

Right there in the church Beatrice broke down in heart-wrenching sobs. She slid out of her pew onto her knees. On bended knee she cried her heart out, for herself, as well as for all of her family, and the turmoil behind the surface of their pretty picture painted lives.

She cried because she was an alcoholic, and only in that very instant had she admitted that to herself. She cried about her very personal loss with the death of Chance Barlow. She cried about the illness of the little girl who got on her nerves, and whose cheeks she always pinched, but whom she knew had the soul of an angel.

Chance's death was enough. They could not lose Jamie too. Her tears were like a dam that had finally broken.

Through her tears all she could see were the fragments of a strange man, from the recurring dream she'd been having since the pre-Christmas breakfast.

Hattie watched her tough, leather-skinned daughter go down on her knees.

She hadn't seen Beatrice on her knees, humbling herself, in honor of the power of the Lord, since she was a child.

Beatrice's voice suddenly soared in the space of the church, with a single prayer, "Father, forgive me for I know not what I do."

"Have your way, Lord," Hattie said. "Have your way."

The twins upon hearing their mother's plea for forgiveness prayed the same prayer gathering around their mother, and Sharese, who was now on her knees praying the same prayer with her mother.

The four poured out their pain, as well as the pain of their flesh, to the Lord in spirit, seeking his love and his mercy, as well as his forgiveness.

Hattie gave an imperceptible nod of her head, to the choir director.

The director lifted her arms. The choir's voices ripped through the church, singing Donnie McClurkin's heartfelt version of "We Fall Down But We Get Up."

Seeing the Brooks clan on their knees in plea to the Lord and knowing the plight of Hattie's great-granddaughter had touched them deep. It had driven their voices to a fever pitch.

They sang, as they progressed in perfect step until they reached the front of the church.

Then there was silence. Total silence.

You couldn't hear even a sniffle from the Brooks clan, all of whom were still on their knees.

In the space of that time the only sound that was heard was *hmmm*.

Then came another nod from Hattie.

A man with a most powerful, deep, velvety baritone voice began to sing:

> *Wading in the water*
> *Wading in the wat-wat-wat-er.*
> *Wading in the water*

The choir jumped in:

Hmmm, hmmm, hmmm, in the water.

The baritone sang in the exact key with which Hattie had been hearing the song in her head.

Hattie leaned on her cane. She walked over to the minister's study room.

It was time.

Outside, police sirens sounded louder and louder as they drew closer to the church.

Hattie kept on walking toward her purpose. She refused to acknowledge or be distracted by the sirens and their meaning.

She opened the door to the study.

George stood with Jamie in his arms. Tears were swimming in his eyes. His whole body trembled.

Jamie's body was hot, blotchy, and unmoving. There was no longer even the rise and fall of her chest.

Dwayne and G-Tang flanked their uncle. Their eyes too were living pools of water and full of grief. G-Tang couldn't get Jamie's voice out of his head. She didn't even look like the Jamie he knew now. Yet, he kept hearing her say, *"I'm just standing here, cuz I love you, G-Tang."*

Now he was standing in church, a place he never expected to find himself, because he *loved* her. He didn't want her to die, though he suspected she was already dead from the way Uncle George was holding her.

There wasn't one sign of life. He even apologized to the Lord for hating Christmas. He asked if he could just bring Jamie back. G-Tang promised the Lord that if he brought Jamie back, he would honor every Christmas he was allowed to see for the rest of his life.

Hattie surveyed the condition of her great-granddaughter. She observed once again the heartbreak in her son's eyes, as well as the reflected pain in her grandsons' eyes.

She got mad.

"Satan, you're a liar," she said, her voice filled with the passion of her feeling.

She nodded, and then turned like a pin on a dime, not missing a step. She moved in an incredibly lithe way for a woman of her advancing age.

The man with the deep baritone voice upped his volume.

> *Wading in the water*
> *Wading in the wat-wat-wat-er.*
> *Wading in the water*

The choir jumped in:

> *Hmmm, hmmm, hmmm, in the water.*

Outside the church the sirens were directly in front now. There was a scrambling of police activity.

Suddenly the sirens were silent.

Hattie led the procession of her family to the baptismal pool. The ones on their knees looked at George carrying Jamie in his arms. They began to cry and pray harder.

Hattie saw the creek. It was directly in front

of her now. She heard the refrain from the song in her head, in addition to the soloist, and the choir's singing.

>*Wading in the water*
>*Wading in the wat-wat-wat-er.*
>*Wading in the water*

The choir jumped in:

>*Hmmm, hmmm, hmmm, in the water.*

She stopped in front of the pool and she turned to her son.

Hattie looked at her precious little darling in George's arms. The little girl with the golden heart. She took her finger, and made the sign of the cross on Jamie's forehead, in the name of Jesus.

"George, give Jamie to the minister."

George hesitated. He didn't want to let go of his granddaughter. Maybe as long as he held her, life would return and she'd be all right. He just didn't know. All he knew was that he didn't want to let her go. He was afraid of what letting her go might mean.

Then he heard the miraculous words that had been spoken to him once before. "George the cancer *is* gone."

Remnants and fragments from his dream, flashed before his eyes.

He handed Jamie over.

"Please, Lord," he prayed under his breath. "Grant us one more miracle."

He gently placed Jamie in the minister's arms.

Lizzie stood in back of George, her heart falling apart as well. She'd cried so much, she felt like an empty well.

She'd called all of their neighbors and friends asking for their prayers for her granddaughter's recovery.

They in turn had called others, until there was an avalanche of phone calls flying through the city, seeking prayer and a Christmas miracle.

The minister took the child in his arms.

Despite what he had been told, he was still surprised at her condition, and the level of heat rising from her body. A heat that he knew would soon be gone, as death settled in.

Her skin literally burned his though, at his mere touching of her. He'd never seen nor heard of anything like it.

He'd been in the ministry going on sixty years. For the first time he knew this would be a night to exhibit faith, in he who was greater than them all. It was time to put it on the line, no more talk.

He signaled the choir director. The singing halted. "Today, family we need to be of great faith and act in one accord. Do you understand?"

People nodded.

"We have to raise our voices to Christ, like we mean it." His voice broke on the last word. Every head in the church nodded, as if they were one.

"Bless you!" the old minister said.

With that he turned to the baptismal pool. He began to slowly lower Jamie's hot, scorching, red-welted body into the water.

The soloist and the choir all sang together now:

Wading in the water
Wading in the wat-wat-wat-er.
Wading in the water
Hmmm, hmmm, hmmm, in the water.

Their voices were a low and steady hum.

Wading in the water

The Brooks clan sang with them:

Wading in the water
Wading in the water

The song had wafted outside the church and down the street, through outside speakers mounted on the church.

Wading in the water

From the neighboring houses surrounding the church, people spilled out of their houses, in their pajamas. All that could be heard was:

Wading in the water

Mr. Mitchell led his own procession of family and friends, which included members of the roundtable and Darryl Payne, as well as scores of other people, walking behind him singing at the top of their voices:

Wading in the water
Wading in the wat-wat-wat-er.
Wading in the water
Hmmm, hmmm, hmmm, in the water.

The police whose job it had been to go inside, and retrieve the sick little girl, bringing her back to the hospital, since she had been spirited out against medical orders, took off their hats, so caught up were they in the spirit of the occasion, and they too began to sing:

> *Wading in the water*
> *Wading in the wat-wat-wat-er.*
> *Wading in the water*
> *Hmmm, hmmm, hmmm, in the water.*

The emergency medical team who arrived in the ambulance to take her back to the hospital sang:

> *Wading in the water*
> *Wading in the wat-wat-wat-er.*
> *Wading in the water*
> *Hmmm, hmmm, hmmm, in the water.*

The people sang in one collective voice, unified.

> *Wading in the water*
> *Wading in the wat-wat-wat-er.*
> *Wading in the water*
> *Hmmm, hmmm, hmmm, in the water.*

There was a presence in the air they had never before felt.

They reached out to the spirit of the Lord, collectively grabbing on to that feeling, tears filling their eyes, and they prayed for the restoration of holiness in their lives.

And, then a wondrous thing happened.

When they remembered holiness, revering it in their hearts, the Spirit of Holiness rose from his burial ground, past the mounds and mounds of dirt he had been buried under, silencing the *ka-chunk*.

Holiness rose like a mighty mountain.

When they embraced the peace they felt, the Soul of Peace who had been stored in the basement of the church, not in the underground of the train station, like the other souls, felt the people's hearts reaching out to him.

They were actually seeking him. And, because they did he left his confinement, and walked among them, spreading himself around, for the first time, in a very long time.

The Soul of Peace was overjoyed when he saw his fellow souls. It had been so long since they had all been together.

The Soul of Love had been awakened from his eternal sleep, when the people had demonstrated love for another outside of themselves, as well as for one another; and he had risen from his slumber, like the sun on a summer day.

The Soul of Hope was there also. He'd felt the people's hearts soaring with the hope of a miracle, once again. As soon as that happened Hope was restored, as they gathered of one spirit, hoping for the recovery of one little child.

The Soul of Redemption literally grabbed the Soul of Forgiveness, hugging him. Because the people's hearts had reached out for forgiveness, he had been able to redeem them before the Lord.

The Soul of Forgiveness's smile was so bright

that it lit the area, as he basked in the tremendous feeling of being wanted.

The underground retreat where the souls had resided sprayed its glorious waters, releasing its gifts, in celebration of the release of the souls.

The only soul missing was Joy.

Inside the church the minister said, "I baptize you in the name of the Lord Jesus Christ, for the remission of your sins."

He lowered Jamie into the water.

He was about to pull her out when Hattie said, "Leave her there."

The voice in which she spoke belied that it was hers. They turned to look at her in unison.

41

In His Name

In the name of Jesus Christ all things are possible unto those whom believe.

"Take your hands away. You no longer have to support her," Hattie said in her own voice now.

The minister removed his hold.

The water supported and rocked Jamie as though she were a tiny baby in a cradle. The waves in the water sung their own lullaby.

Jamie's inner eyes had been *watching* for God.

She knew she'd heard his voice saying, "*Come near my child. Come near to me.*"

All of her focus was on the sound of that voice. Her inner eye watched for the Lord Jesus Christ. Though her body was tormented, her spirit soared.

Then she heard Jesus, singing:

Wading in the water
Wading in the wat-wat-wat-er.
Wading in the water
Hmmm, hmmm, hmmm, in the water.

It was the most beautiful sound she had ever heard. He was singing to her. She knew it. Her heart soared as she recognized his voice. She had heard that voice before, and she knew it was his. Jamie's body continued to float on top of the water.

Then a strange thing happened.

The water splashed around her. Glistening drops of water shot to the ceiling, looking like sprays of crystal. The water then fell in a spray of glistening crystalline drops. It distributed the misty droplets of water all over Jamie's still face and body.

Slowly she opened her eyes. Her body dipped, immersing fully in the water.

Then she was floating again.

"Now," was all Hattie said as she once again saw the creek.

The minister gently lifted Jamie from the baptismal pool, with a normal body temperature. There wasn't a red welt in sight. There was not the slightest sign of illness or sickness, on this child.

Jamie came out of the water singing, just as Jesus had sung to her:

Wading in the water
Wading in the wat-wat-wat-er.
Wading in the water
Hmmm, hmmm, hmmm, in the water.

Upon spotting Hattie she gave her a bright smile, "Hi, Grandma!"

The old woman broke down in tears.

All of the people who could fit surged into the church; others crowded the streets, outside its doors.

Hattie whispered a suggestion to the minister renewing his feeling once again that she'd always been a great asset to the church.

"I'd like us all . . ." the minister's voice boomed with love, the excitement of miracles, and enthusiasm. "While we're gathered here, I'd like us all to kneel and pray for the youth of our city, as one voice. After prayer we're going to organize in groups, and take action to deal with this situation. We are no longer going to stand idly by, and lose our children. It is up to us to do something about it."

The woman who had lost her grandson kissed Hattie's cheek. The mothers' of the murdered boys in the city who were also in attendance, and had met under the direst circumstances of rage and murder, embraced each other crying at those words, and the expressions of agreement on the people's faces.

Their sons' lives would now not be lost in vain. Perhaps some good could come of their deaths, in having people take a serious look at the situation, as well as preventing the death of others.

The one angel looked at the other, as the blood from his footprints, still traceable in the streets from the night when the boys had originally been murdered, disappeared.

The other angel just smiled.

"Let us join hands," the minister said.

They did. All of them, from the church to the streets, they linked hands and acted as one.

A gap had been bridged.

Jamie

Jamie sat on the edge of the baptismal pool staring at the water in which she had been healed.

"Thank you, Jesus, I love you. You have a nice singing voice, too!" she said.

She stuck her hand in the water, seeing Cynthia's image, and whispered, "Jesus, please bring my mommy home. I believe!"

Then she'd gone downstairs, with the great innocence that only children seemed to possess, for juice and snacks.

Her heart had always been desirous of being with her mother. Yet, now she had an even bigger wish. She wanted Cynthia to be a part of the huge Christmas Eve celebration at the church.

She didn't want her mother to miss out on such an important event. It was going to be so special. The congregation—and others—instead of cooking, baking, and celebrating at home, had agreed to celebrate Christ's birth as one family in the church.

The gift of *one love* was what they would be giving.

There were going to be scores of people celebrating holiness. Not everyone would fit in the church, so there would be tables and tents all up and down the block and the surrounding streets.

It had become exceptionally warm for this time of the year, and Christmas Eve was to bring record warmth, according to the weather reports.

People in the surrounding houses were throwing open their doors, just as the church was, in welcome of the coming festivities.

They'd never felt so good about Christmas, nor so excited about the celebration of it. They had received the gift of renewed hope and faith. They remembered the Christ Child's birth, and the reason for the greatest love of all:

That God had given his only begotten son, so that whomsoever believed in him would be saved.

They knew love didn't get any greater than that. Not one of them would have had the capacity to watch their child suffer and die for the good of others.

In total grace and mercy their reminder had been Christ's deliverance of one little girl, one of their own.

Jamie.

It was time to give the Lord Jesus Christ his just due.

43

Cynthia

Drip. Drip. Drip. It was back. It was the most comforting sound she'd ever heard. She'd felt almost naked without the sound of it. What once had been annoying, slowly, over time had become comforting.

The prison had finally emerged from the mysterious blackout and had light.

Cynthia didn't care why the lights went out. For the first time in her life she had spent her time in the dark for good—praying.

She was comforted from her prayer. As such she had received renewed hope. She didn't care what they knew or didn't know. She now knew what she knew, and that was a fact.

She picked up the picture of Jamie, just as a guard showed up summoning her.

"What did I do now?" she ask defensively.

"Your counselor wants to see you."

Cynthia huffed her way past the guard wondering what other annoyance they had in store for her now.

It was Christmas. Couldn't they just leave her alone? If she couldn't be at home, at least she could be left in peace.

Once she was settled in the counselor's office, she pulled her knees up to her chin, waiting for the bomb to drop.

The counselor gave her a level stare.

Cynthia Brooks was one of the most trying prisoners she had ever had. The woman had worn out her reserves with her rebellious attitude, quickness to fight, and her penchant for game and hustling people.

A smile touched the counselor's lips.

Cynthia rolled her eyes knowing that wasn't good. She knew the counselor was sick of her. She had probably figured out a way to transfer her to another prison, the equivalent of Siberia or something. As if the Danbury federal prison wasn't enough.

"Cynthia, you're going home."

Cynthia sat mute. She didn't feel like playing with this woman. She rolled her eyes again.

"You're going home for Christmas."

Cynthia unwillingly sniffled. She'd rather be back in the hole, than have her feelings played with.

The counselor shook her head, as she observed Cynthia's lack of response, realizing that Cynthia either hadn't heard her or didn't believe a word she'd said.

She walked from behind her desk and stood in front of Cynthia. In an authoritative, official voice designed to penetrate the wall surrounding Cynthia she said, "At 12 noon on December 24th, Christmas Eve day, which is tomorrow, Cynthia Brooks, you will be released from the Danbury federal penitentiary, a free woman, as time served."

Drip. Drip. Drip.

Jamie's voice sang softly, "*Wading in the water.*"

Hattie's voice:

> *Wading in the water*
> *Wading in the wat-wat-wat-er.*
> *Wading in the water*
> *Hmmm, hmmm, hmmm, in the water.*

Her grandmother's voice finished the song.

The dripping turned to song, and it filled her heart. Her sorrow turned to comfort, and it filled her mind. Her despair turned into hope, and it filled her soul. Hope, in all its brightness, shone from her eyes.

Almost afraid to look up Cynthia peered through her long lashes, a Brooks family trait, to look up at the woman.

She finally saw the truth reflected in her eyes. Cynthia rose from her chair.

"It's true," Sylvia said handing her the release paper.

"You're going to be home with your baby girl for Christmas," her voice dropped to the lowest of whispers, as she watched the seal of street game stripped away to reveal the real woman Cynthia was.

Emerging was a beautiful woman of both spirit and flesh. The counselor had never witnessed this side of Cynthia, nor had she ever known it was even there.

Cynthia whispered the words this time. "I'm going home," she said disbelievingly. Then, "I'm going home," she said more strongly. Finally, "I'm going home!" she shouted.

"There's no place like home," she shrieked. She almost felt like clicking her heels, the same as Dorothy had in the *Wizard of Oz*. Except you couldn't click paper slippers that were made in a prison. Nevertheless, she could jump up and down, and that she did.

She hugged the counselor. Sylvia returned her hug, knowing full well in her twenty-five years of service in the penal system, she'd never seen, not even once, a prisoner released on Christmas Eve Day. It was unheard of.

For Cynthia the dripping had turned to song. When the dripping had stopped, it was time for her to go home.

The Soul of Peace perched on the windowsill, filling Cynthia's heart with his gift of peace. The first she'd had in her entire life.

Though she wasn't physically there, she would not miss out, on the Brooks family's blessings.

It bears mentioning that before the beginning of time, the Lord's face was on the deep, of the water.

> *Wading in the water*
> *Wading in the wat-wat-wat-er.*
> *Wading in the water*
> *Hmmm, hmmm, hmmm, in the water.*

44

The Gift of Family

Each member of the Brooks family had gone home to retrieve enough personal belongings for the two-night stay at George's house.

George had a second floor in his house.

Although it was rare that anyone ever used this floor, it was like a page out of *House Beautiful*, decorated by courtesy of Lizzie with her fine eye for all things beautiful.

Staying in a guest room at George's was the equivalent of being put up in a country breakfast inn, at its most plush.

The family had all descended on George's house, because it had been decided that they all needed more family time together. More than they could get if they were each running back to their own homes.

Hattie shared a large room with Beatrice, who at fifty-nine suddenly had the urge to be near her mother. Sharese and Georgette shared a room. This gave them time to catch up on sistah talk; since both of their lives were so busy that this rarely ever happened.

George, G-Tang, and Dwayne bunked together, leaving one bedroom free.

Lizzie was in her heyday with the house full of love and family. This was a dream come true for her, because this is exactly what she'd always felt family should be like—love, caring, and sharing.

Who could have too much of that?

Jamie was right by her Grandma Lizzie's side, smiling and happy. Lizzie turned to Jamie while pulling out a family favorite, a casserole of baked okra, corn, and tomato.

Lizzie smiled at the music, warmth of laughter, and teasing rivalry she heard coming from the family gathered in the living room.

"Jamie, are you sure you haven't seen my extra place setting? I've been looking all over for it!"

"No, Grandma Lizzie, it was here for the pre-Christmas breakfast."

Lizzie placed the casserole on top of the stove, covering it. She put her hands on her hips in thought, contemplating. "You're right. It was."

She pointed to the shelf it was usually housed on. "But look, it isn't there, now."

She frowned again. She reached into her second oven to pull out a sweet potato pie, with its fragrant scent of cinnamon, butter, and nutmeg wafting through the air.

As soon as the pie was removed from the oven one of the twins raced into the kitchen.

Lizzie laughed when she bumped into George who was right on her elbow. "Auntie Lizzie," he said trying to sweeten her up. "You know I'm the taste tester."

"Boy, this pie has got to cool before you can eat it." She sat it on the cooling rack.

George looked heavenward. "If you insist." He grabbed some snowball cookies off the cookie platter.

"You're impossible," Lizzie laughed. He popped one of them in his mouth, closing his eyes in ecstasy.

"I want some cookies too, Grandma," Jamie piped up. "George has some."

George pecked her on the forehead. "I'm grown. You can't do what I do."

Handing Jamie cookies, she said, "You can't do what you do." They all laughed.

The phone rang. Lizzie wiped her hands on her apron. She reached for it. "Hello."

Her expression went from warmth, to curious, to disbelief, to scared confusion, in the flash of a second.

"George!" Lizzie screamed. "George!" Her husband came running.

George and Jamie each froze, cookies forgotten, as they watched in astonished disbelief as tears flowed down Lizzie's cheeks.

She had gone from laughter to tears in the space of a few seconds.

"What!" George's heart pounded as he stood

there looking at her. Lizzie never screamed like that. Good God, what else could go wrong?

Saying not a word, unable to speak if she'd wanted to she simply handed him the phone. Her tears continued to flow. Her hand trembled.

"Thank you, Jesus. Thank you, Jesus. Thank you, Jesus," she uttered, finally finding her voice.

By now the whole family was standing in the kitchen while George hugged his Lizzie close to him with one arm, and cradled the phone with his other.

"Mr. Brooks, I'm Claude Brown calling from the Danbury federal prison in regards to your daughter, Cynthia Brooks," the voice on the phone said in a no-nonsense official tone.

George's heart skipped a beat, as he thought about all the horror stories he'd heard about prison. All those thoughts crowded in his mind blocking out any sense of reasoning.

Please God, don't let anything have happened to my daughter. Please, Lord Jesus. George prayed, silently.

The voice of Claude Brown went on, completely unaware of the trauma he had caused on the other end of the phone. "Ms. Cynthia Brooks is officially being released tomorrow on December 24th at 12 noon with time served. Mr. Brooks, your daughter will be a free woman."

George whooped so loudly he almost didn't hear the man's request to pick Cynthia up. Dear Lord, he hadn't thought it was possible, but it was. They had all been wrong, Cynthia was coming home.

The voice finally penetrated his fog with a request to gather Cynthia from the prison the following day. "Yes! Yes, I can, and I will!"

George hung up. The entire family was silent, all watching him, holding their collective breaths, not daring to believe.

In that instant all George saw was his granddaughter, looking at him, a curious expression across her features.

Lizzie's sniffle was the only sound heard.

My God, George thought, this is certainly a Christmas full of miracles. Lizzie had told him so, and he didn't believe. All we need is a miracle, she'd kept saying.

They'd wanted only one, and that was for Cynthia to come home for Christmas. Yet, they had received an avalanche of them.

He let go of Lizzie, reaching for his grandchild. Everyone waited, in suspenseful silence.

He picked Jamie up, looked deep into her eyes, proud that he was going to be the one to deliver her very special Christmas present.

"Jamie."

"Yes, Granddaddy?" Jamie looked at him with doe-like eyes, fear striking her heart for an instant. Then she remembered her grandmother's words. "No matter what, you've got to believe."

She smiled brightly as she glanced over at Hattie.

Then she heard the voice singing.

Hmmm, hmmm, hmmm, in the water.

In that space of time she knew Jesus hadn't let her down.

"Your Mommy will be home for Christmas, and for Christmas Eve! We're going to pick her up tomorrow."

The family let out a loud cheer.

Jamie Lynne Brooks burst into tears.

45

Secrets Laid to Rest

Since it had been decided that the entire family as one unit would pick Cynthia up from Danbury, the volume of work had to be seriously stepped up.

Long into the evening they all helped Lizzie with cooking and baking so they could get the food over to the church for the Christmas Eve celebration, as well as prepare their own Christmas lunch and dinner, with the exception of the last-minute items, like Lizzie's famous macaroni and cheese casserole, a family favorite.

They talked and shared more than they ever had before, laying some secrets to rest.

Dwayne not realizing the extent to which his sister would be devastated and hurt when he had used her as a confessional in the museum, decided to make an arrangement that would ease her mind. He was both contrite and sorry for the intrusion he had made on her life.

So he arranged a very private, special conversation for her after severing his relationship with the CEO of her company. It was one step at a time, but he was on the road to recovery.

During this conversation Sharese was assured that all was fine, and that each had made the appropriate arrangements to seek the guidance they each needed.

Sharese went to her brother, for the first time seeing, as well as acknowledging, his personal pain and agony, and how he had lived with that painful secret, unable to share it, for a good deal of time.

She decided to try to understand his life from his point of view. They both decided to love more, respect more, and protect one another more, going forward as family should.

In turn Dwayne would help her through her personal crisis, part of which was identity, and where her place really was in life.

He had already begun to help her, by listening, really listening, to the inner Sharese, as they sat by Uncle George's fireplace on the upper floor of the house alone, talking about everything under the sun.

He listened fully tuning in an ear, to the inner Sharese, not the outer Sharese, giving her his shoulder to lean on, as she needed it. In that time they both learned the importance of giving to others what one wanted to receive for themselves.

The twins were going to be baptized on Christmas Eve, arranged by their grandmother once they had shared with her how far they had strayed away from the Lord, on a dark and dangerous path that they no longer wanted to be on.

Hattie never judged them. She simply said, "Jesus Christ can save anybody."

Then she arranged for their baptism, during the celebration of Christ's birth on Christmas Eve.

G-Tang and Beatrice finally talked, really talked about Chance Barlow's life and death, as well as their own lives.

G-Tang admitted that he hated Christmas, and how he had come to love, and understand Christmas more, during Jamie's illness.

He then showed Beatrice something special that he'd found in the box in the attic. That box had been haunting him, so he had finally gone into the attic to open it. The day he opened it there was no music playing from the attic.

He showed Beatrice a picture of the three of them, Chance, Beatrice, and him, when he was a little boy at Christmas time. There was a strange handwriting on it at the bottom, in Chance's scribble. It read:

> *I'll always love you both, and I always have.*
> *Merry Christmas!*
> *Chance*
> *For you G-Tang it's Daddy!*

Beatrice shivered. The picture trembled in her hand.

She knew the handwriting and it was Chance's. She also knew it couldn't have been there before, because when David was a little boy, he'd never gone by the nickname of G-Tang. He had acquired that particular moniker as a teenager. Also, Chance had been locked up ever since David acquired that name, and had never once sent a picture of any type to their house.

Beatrice hugged G-Tang close to her. She decided to tell him that she had decided to quit drinking. They had much to live for, and she didn't want to see it, or not see it, because she was in a drunken haze.

She no longer wanted to disrespect herself, or her son anymore by falling out drunk on the couch with a bottle of J&B.

Beatrice was as good as her word. From that day forward she never took another drink. She fought alcoholism the same way she had fought hard in the streets. She fought to win.

George had a private moment with his mother.

The turn of events had touched his heart in a place he hadn't visited too often. He decided to share his miracle, with her. His voice still held the awe of his experience.

When he'd finished, Hattie had patted his hand, saying, "I know. Jesus healed you."

George had looked at her in surprise.

"Baby," Hattie had said as though he were still a child. "I been serving Jesus Christ ever since I waded in the creek water, and was baptized, many moons ago. The Lord rewards those who are faithful!"

She took his hand in hers. "Do you know the history of the song, 'Wade in De Water'?"

George shook his head in the negative.

"That song is an old negro spiritual that contained carefully coded instructions to assist the slaves in finding their way to freedom."

Hattie sighed looking off into the distance, as though she could see the slaves listening to the song, and running to freedom.

"That song has roots in the slaves escaping via the Underground Railroad." She coughed clearing her throat. It was a quite racking cough that shook her whole body.

George glanced at her concerned.

She waved his concern away, her voice returning to full throttle. "I believe the Lord put that song on my heart in this particular time, what we like to call contemporary times, in order to lead us to freedom once again."

She went totally silent, and then leaned forward, staring into the depths of her son's eyes. Her look was so deep that she literally saw the bottom well of his eyes. "This time he's *using* it to lead us to our spiritual freedom. There are all kinds of bondages, George. Not all of them contain chains that we can see."

George experienced the chill of her words in his spirit. That chill prickled up and down his spine.

"Do you understand?"

George nodded. She then took him fully into her arms, cradling him against her bosom, as he cried.

Hattie's heart swelled with pride.

Jesus Christ had come through for her, and her family. She had been serving him since she was a girl, running barefoot by the creek, and for this he had rewarded her.

The family's hearts and secrets had been laid to rest. It was time to celebrate, Christmas Eve, and right on its heels, the greatest day of all, Christmas!

Christmas Eve

George's Escalade allowed them to transport everything they needed to the church in one trip before leaving to pick Cynthia up.

They looked like a caravan since it had taken a few vehicles to transport everyone comfortably. At the stroke of noon, as promised, Cynthia Brooks walked out of the Danbury federal prison, a free woman.

Jamie was so overwhelmed to finally see her mother that she just stood there looking at her, tears shimmering in her eyes, unable to move.

Cynthia's throat tightened. She touched her daughter's cheek before hugging her, as if she'd never let her go.

In Cynthia's eyes Jamie had seen a new Cynthia, and she knew things would be different for her and her mother from now on. Her mother wasn't the same person who had gone to prison.

She was of a different spirit, as well as of a different mind-set. She even moved differently.

This change didn't escape Hattie's notice, either. She just looked up to the sky, thinking what an amazing Savior, Jesus Christ really was.

It was a shame more people didn't know it.

The Spirit of Innocence said to the Spirit of Discernment. "I'm glad she's able to go home. Jamie missed her so much!"

"So true, little one," Discernment responded.

But as Sam watched Cynthia a new and dawning realization came his way. His heart grew heavy with the weight of it, as well as heavy with the many lessons he had learned.

Looking up at Discernment he said in a quiet tone, "It's almost time for me to go. Isn't it?"

The Spirit of Discernment had anticipated this heartbreaking question from Sam. "Yes, Sam, it is."

Sam continued to watch the Brooks clan, hugging, kissing, and really listening to one another, while embracing the true concept of family in their excitement.

"Jamie doesn't need me anymore," he observed, while realizing just how much the Brooks family had changed.

Discernment chuckled softly. "Sure she does, little one," he said affectionately. "You'll just watch over her from afar, now."

His love was so pure that Discernment knew the Spirit of Innocence, despite some tough lessons and his training to be the wisest little angel in his innocence, would always be just that, innocent.

It was a trait that would be intact for him throughout eternity.

The thought was a comforting one.

After many tears, hugs, kisses, and exchanges of jackets, as well as packages of new clothes for Cynthia, so she could shed her old clothing, they all headed to the church.

When they got within a mile of the church inside the city limits of Hartford, they realized something was very wrong.

"What's going on?" George wondered aloud. There was gridlock. Cell phone calls were flying from car to car, but no one knew what was going on.

They were stuck in a virtual parking lot, and it wasn't moving. Period. They were at a standstill.

A young police officer they had seen in church, pulled up on the side of George's truck.

Spotting Jamie in the backseat next to her mother, he said, "Hi, precious."

"Merry Christmas, Mr. Freeman," Jamie said.

"Merry Christmas to you, too, angel girl," he said, surprised that she knew his name.

George wasn't surprised. That was just the nature of his precocious granddaughter. She had been treating them to some of the most amazing poetry, on the trip from Danbury, as she dazzled her mother with all of her newly developed word skills.

"What's going on?" George asked the officer.

Spying Hattie on the other side of the truck, the officer broke out in a grin.

"Your family has started something, Mr.

Brooks. All these people are here because of that. They're here to celebrate Christ's birth as part of the church's Christmas Eve celebration. I guess word gets around."

George was dumbfounded, as he looked at all those people, a whole sea of them. "You're kidding!"

"No, sir. I'm not. This is Jesus Day!"

His partner chirped in. "You're never going to get there in your vehicles. Just leave them here, and lock them up. The area hospitals have lent their helicopters to airlift you and your family to the church."

"My, my, my," Hattie said.

"Grandma, we're gonna fly!" Jamie shouted excitedly.

"On the wings of glory, baby; you'd better believe that."

Lizzie was already on the phone relaying the news to the rest of the family. It was a Christmas Eve celebration that went down in the annals of Hartford's history.

Throngs of people all of goodwill and good cheer. Hallelujah!

Once they reached the church there was prayer service, singing, fellowship, and baptisms. The twins weren't the only ones to get baptized.

Beatrice and G-Tang decided to wade in the water too.

G-Tang had promised to enter rehabilitation in exchange for Beatrice's withdrawal from the bottle.

Quite a lot of people were baptized in the name of Jesus Christ. There were lines of them, crowding the streets, waiting for their chance to wade in the water, just as their ancestors had so long ago.

All of the people were whispering and talking about the miraculous recovery of one little girl, and they wanted to know about this man called Jesus, who was responsible for making her well again.

They reasoned if Jesus had done it for her, he would do it for them, so they lined up for their blessing. And not one person would go without. The doors of that church wouldn't close until the last person who wanted to be baptized was.

Christmas Eve came to a true spiritual full circle when every single man, woman, and child lifted a lit candle for the Lord Jesus Christ as a mass of people united as one, in his name and because of his birth.

The people all blew the candles out, uniting as one to pray for the slain youth and the loss of their children.

On the heels of that the lights went out. The city of Hartford plunged into a total blackout. Not one person saw the hand that blocked the lights.

When the lights came back on there was a quiet hush.

The only sound that could be heard was *hmmm!*

47

Christmas Day

Christmas Day dawned early, very early, for the Brooks family.

At precisely 4 A.M. Jamie awakened. Rubbing the sleep from her eyes she looked over and smiled at her sleeping mother, glad to feel the warmth from her body next to her.

Just like they used to do, regardless of the lateness of the hour every Christmas Eve, Cynthia had smuggled some of Lizzie's fresh-baked cookies and a glass of milk into Jamie's room for a late-night snack to be shared between them.

They had giggled mischievously, as if they were both children at their misbehavior. Jamie snuggled closer to her mother, content to have her near.

She tried to go back to sleep, but she couldn't because something was off-kilter. Tossing and turning for a while she finally decided to get out of bed.

She listened intently.

She couldn't hear any people noises. In fact, she realized with a small shock, she couldn't hear any noises at all. It was as if a blanket of hush had been thrown over the house. Not even Grand-daddy's usual snoring could be heard.

Sam giggled as he watched Jamie puzzling over the silence.

Discernment situated his robes glancing at Cynthia who was still sleeping after her over-whelming homecoming.

Jamie frowned then decided to pad over to sit on her window seat, to look out of the window.

As much as she yearned to wake up her mother, she didn't because she knew she was probably exhausted.

Grabbing one of her favorite stuffed animals courtesy of Sharese, she curled up in the window seat cuddling the soft bear, and looked out of the window.

Her eyes widened.

Sam laughed out loud. Jamie's shrieks of pure joy woke up all of the family. They heard the shrieking and descended on Jamie and Cynthia's room.

"What in tarnation?" George asked, sounding a bit like his mother, caught up in Jamie's excitement.

Jamie was jumping up and down, much like her spiritual counterpart Sam did when he was either agitated or caught in a web of excitement.

Jamie ran to her grandfather. She pulled him to the window. Cynthia tried to focus, on her daughter, and the growing crowd in the room, while wiping the sleep from her eyes.

"Look, Granddaddy. Look!" Jamie pointed out the window. Sure enough there were piles of huge soft white snowflakes, falling gently from the sky.

The ground was fully covered in a blanket of glistening snow.

There was a beautiful hush in the air that embraced them enveloping them in peace.

Silent night! Holy night! All is calm. All is bright, the heavenly choir breathed softly.

Sam's laughter grew into a beautiful sound when the Soul of Joy entered the room. He had been the only soul who hadn't yet awakened. His appearance was the culmination of all things.

Joy saluted Discernment and Sam as the Brooks family hugged one another, staring out the window in awe.

He then took his leave, going to spread himself around, to the hearts and minds of other people in the city.

The heavenly choir struck a song that spoke directly to the occasion, *Joy to the world! The Lord has come! Let earth receive her King! Let every heart prepare him room, and heaven and nature sing, and heaven and nature sing. And heaven, and nature sing!*

Jamie said, "See. I told people it was going to snow! All I had to do was believe. Right, Grandma?"

"That's right, baby!" Hattie said leaning on her cane.

The phone rang. It was Mr. Mitchell. Lizzie put him on the speakerphone, as she did all the guests who called for Christmas, every year.

"I knew you guys were up. Merry Christmas!"

A chorus of Merry Christmases followed his greeting.

"Jamie?"

"Yes, Mr. Mitchell?"

"Did you know that it's snowing outside?"

Jamie giggled. "Yes, Mr. Mitchell."

"Okay. I was just checking," Mr. Mitchell said before laughing, and hanging up.

What a special child she is, he thought.

Next came the phone call from Old Man Barlow, who was promptly invited to spend Christmas Day and have Christmas dinner with the Brooks family, so he could spend some time with his grandson, G-Tang, a walking replica of the son he'd just lost.

Old Man Barlow happily accepted. Joy filled his heart.

The Soul of Joy waved at Sam and Discernment, a last time. He had been hovering near the door, before leaving.

"Jamie!" Cydney's voice was the next one to boom over the speakerphone, in childlike excitement. "I'm glad you're well. Merry Christmas!"

"Thank you, Cydney. Merry Christmas to you too!"

The whole street knew the family was up because as was their tradition, they turned on all the lights—inside and outside—every Christmas when they arose.

Jamie turned to her Grandma Lizzie now. "Grandma Lizzie, Cydney missed her pre-Christmas breakfast with us, because I was sick. Can she come today?"

"Absolutely," Lizzie smiled.

"Cydney are you in the mood for some Christmas morning French toast, and hot chocolate with whipped cream?"

"You bet I am, Mrs. Brooks!" Cydney's excitement bubbled over the phone.

"Okay, bring your Mom too and we'll see you at 9 A.M. sharp for breakfast."

The last sound they heard was Cydney yelling, "Mommy! Can we have breakfast at Mrs. Brooks' house?" And, she knew they would, because no one ever turned down an invitation to sit at Lizzie's table.

It really wasn't just the food.

There was a real sense of family and presence as well as genuine love and care in the way Lizzie prepared meals, and people in the same way that sheep flocked to their shepherd's call responded to that, and were drawn to that love.

Cynthia snuggled in the window seat, leaning her head against the window, and pulling Jamie on her lap, watching the gently falling snow, while counting her blessings.

Hattie sighed. She turned to the two angels for a second, crossing over into their realm, a realm in which the rest of her family wasn't privy to.

She leaned over to kiss Sam, on his forehead. Then she whispered in his ear. "Thank you for watching over my great-granddaughter."

She winked at the Spirit of Discernment.

Sam nearly fainted from the shock of it, and then he stumbled over his feet, and blushed. He'd never really believed the old woman could see them at times, but apparently she could.

Her faith had transcended their realm, that's

how she'd been able to see, and now it was that same faith that had enabled her to kiss him.

Discernment regally bowed his good-bye to the old woman who represented a tower of faith and strength.

Sam went over to stand near Jamie who was cradled in her mother's arms, and the wisest little angel in training wrapped his arms around the both of them briefly, before planting a kiss on Jamie's nose.

As Discernment and Hattie looked on, Sam ran his fingers lovingly down Jamie's face. He would miss her in this realm, but he knew he'd never be far away from her.

With that last gesture the angels took their leave. Discernment reached for Sam's hand, and they were gone.

But by far the grandest moment of Christmas occurred, when Sam looked over, as he listened to the heavenly Angel Choir singing, "Joy to the world. The Lord has come. Let Earth receive her king!"

He looked over to see the Lord Jesus Christ, looking down upon the Earth, and smiling.

After all it was *his* birthday.

And the Spirit whispered, "And his name shall be called Emmanuel!" Behold a virgin shall be with child, and shall bring forth a son, and they shall call his name Em-man'-u-el, which being interpreted is, God with us.

Dear Readers:

I'd like you to know that the writing of *The Forgotten Spirit* marks a historical time in the spirit for me. Please know that no gift in the spirit is without sacrifice. This story truly is the greatest gift that I have to give.

Jesus Christ gave the greatest gift of all. His life.

Amen!

Evie Rhodes

Mailing address:
Evie Rhodes
P.O. Box 320503
Hartford, CT 06132

Email:
Evierhodes@Evierhodes.com
Web Site:
www.Evierhodes.com

Look For These Other
Dafina Novels